TROUBLE *in Tucson*

ACKNOWLEGEMENTS:
I want to thank all the people that helped me get this anthology started and finished.
Sharon Browning
Sally Marquingy
Kathy McIntosh
Lynn Nicholas
Elaine A. Powers
Cheryl Ryan – cover art
Kate Joy Steele

TROUBLE *in Tucson*

AN ANTHOLOGY BY MEMBERS OF
TUCSON SISTERS IN CRIME
DESERT SLEUTHS
&
SISTERS IN CRIME GRAND CANYON WRITERS
FOR
LEFT COAST CRIME 2023

EVA ELDRIDGE, EDITOR

Published by Lyric Power Publishing, LLC Tucson AZ
Lyricpower.net

Cover design by Cheryl Ryan
Cherylryan.com

ISBN: 979-8-375928-05 0

Contents

TROUBLE *in Tucson*

INTRODUCTION

EVA ELDRIDGE

Tucson is the place I belong. It's where my heart resides. When the idea of an anthology entitled "Trouble in Tucson" was suggested for Left Coast Crime, I was intrigued. This area is a mixture of good and bad, heat and cold, beauty and the ugly underbelly. Tales about what kind of trouble we can find in Tucson was the right tool to pluck my heartstrings.

As I worked my way through the submissions, I looked for stories that covered a range of subjects, emotions, and situations. We have stories about murder, of course. Murder being one of the ultimate forms of trouble. We have stories about longing and coveting what others have. We have stories that make you think about things we don't want to talk about and stories that will make you laugh. I hope the resulting assortment will entertain you and leave you thinking about a number of troubling things.

All of the stories submitted to this anthology were submitted by the members of Sisters in Crime, the Arizona chapters: Tucson Sisters in Crime, Desert Sleuths, and Sisters in Crime Grand Canyon Writers. I want to thank every person who submitted a story because I enjoyed reading them all. Unfortunately, I couldn't fit them all into this anthology. I wanted to. Please enjoy Trouble in Tucson.

~*~

112 IN THE SHADE

SUSAN CUMMINS MILLER

Tucson, Arizona, Saturday, June 25

One hundred and twelve degrees in the shade. Forty percent humidity. Not a breath of breeze. Pima County Homicide Detective Toni Navarro ran a handkerchief over her face and adjusted her hat.

Although normally a dry month, the monsoon rains had arrived on June 24, El Día de San Juan, the feast day of St. John the Baptist. The traditional beginning of the summer planting and gathering season for the local Tohono O'odham. And the early storm wasn't a fluke. Monsoon clouds again mushroomed in the southern sky.

Thorns snagged Toni's pant legs as she forged a path through a thicket and down the bank of Sabino Creek. Sycamores grew along the damp wash, their white bark dappled with shade like an appaloosa's flank.

Scott Munger, Toni's partner, checked the GPS on his cell. "Almost there. Should be hearing the recovery crew."

It was too hot to talk. In silence they followed the wash as it dog-legged upstream. Evidence of yesterday's flashflood abounded. A railroad tie lodged ten feet up in a cottonwood. Tufts of dry grass draped catclaw and creosote. Strand lines of

3

black mica traced the contours of the arroyo's edge. Nearby, a curve-billed thrasher whistled from a staghorn cholla.

Around the bend they found the recovery unit. Toni and Scott slipped on booties and masks. The Medical Examiner moved aside to allow them access. The water's force had stripped away several feet of the bank, exposing scarlet cloth. A hollow under the gnarled roots of a velvet mesquite cradled the remains. The woman had been buried hastily, probably last fall or winter when the creek was dry. The killer had caved in the bank to conceal the body. Winter precipitation hadn't been plentiful enough to strip away the earth cover.

Toni crouched beside the remains. The end of a leg bone protruded. A few strands of long, dark-blonde hair lay twisted among the sand grains. The skull had been crushed by something heavy, though that damage might have been postmortem.

She stepped back to allow Munger a closer view. A rock, he suggested. The M.E. grunted that they could wait for the autopsy results.

The forensics crew placed the corpse gently in a body bag, leaving it unzipped. The dress, an expensive silk sheath, had held up better than the body. A gold pin with a Mimbres basket design still clung to the cloth at her right shoulder. A sunbeam glanced over the concave, circular surface. Toni had seen that workmanship before, somewhere . . .

"It's JoJo Dixon." The pronouncement came from the shadows under a sycamore.

Frankie MacFarlane was sitting like an ascetic Buddha, legs crossed, back propped against the trunk, writing in a notebook. She taught geological sciences at Foothills Community College, a short distance away. They'd known each other since high school. JoJo Dixon had been their classmate.

Tony shivered as her mind superimposed the memory of JoJo's face and hair on the remains of the skull. "Hey, Frankie. You found her?"

"As luck would have it. I was prepping a lesson on chanel erosion and sedimentation." Frankie stood and stretched to her full six-foot height. "I've had ninety minutes to deal with the shock." She tore a few pages from her notebook. "I wrote up my notes. Permission to join you?"

Scott traded a pair of booties for her notes. "You sure about the ID, Frankie?"

"She's sure about that gold pin," Toni said. "Jojo's father gave it to her when she graduated from high school. It had belonged to her mother. Frankie and I were both there when she opened the present."

Frankie jumped down to the creek bed and said to Munger, "Full name, Josephine Joyce Dixon. But everyone called her JoJo. She taught Art and Art History at FCC. Specialized in fabric art. And she was wearing that dress and pin at the holiday party on December tenth. That was the last time Philo or I saw her."

Philo Dain was Frankie's fiancé. Tucson was a small town. Everyone was at most two degrees of separation away from everyone else. Toni's husband had died rescuing Philo after a helicopter crash years before. Philo and Toni co-owned a couple of properties.

"She was heading to Italy the next morning," Frankie said. "An eight-month sabbatical in Florence. She wasn't due back till August."

"That's a long time to be incommunicado without anyone noticing," Scott said.

"JoJo didn't have a partner or significant other," Frankie said. "There was only her father. Her mother died the summer after our freshman year of high school."

"I remember," Toni said. "After she lost her mother, JoJo closed down."

"She kept her distance from me, too, even though we'd known each other since preschool," Frankie said. "I made one overture when we both got hired at FCC, but she fobbed me off. And she was famous for shutting down her phone and computer when she was out of the country. That said, if she hadn't posted her class grades, someone would have noticed. So she must have done that before the party."

"Is her father still around?"

"I think so."

Toni made a couple of notes. "Did JoJo bring a date to the party?"

"There was someone—Philo spoke to him."

"Anything memorable about that night?"

"You could say that," said a man's voice.

Both Toni and Scott stopped writing. The Scene-of-Crimes team paused. A raven landed noisily in a cottonwood, jarring at them. And Philo Dain appeared at Frankie's side.

"I wish you'd stop doing that." Toni handed him booties.

"You'd worry if I made noise," Philo said, stretching the fabric over his cross-trainers.

He glanced at the remains, but didn't move closer. Nor did he seem curious. But Toni knew that Philo, retired Special Forces and the owner of Dain Investigations, noticed everything.

"Soon as I realized it was JoJo, I called Philo." Frankie slipped her hand into his. "Figured whoever handled this case would need his statement."

"Ladies first," Philo said.

"Okay. The party was memorable because JoJo's students pranked her. And JoJo went ballistic."

"Explain," said Toni and Scott together.

***

Later, typing up her report, Toni marveled at the strange twists a life could take.

Frankie had related details of last December's FCC soirée as if she were living it. The students in Dixon's Fabric Arts class, who'd been tasked with making centerpieces for the tables, had exercised artistic license by arranging Santa, Mrs. Claus, the elves and reindeer in compromising positions. The handmade elves were not on shelves—they were on each other. And on reindeer, Santa, and Mrs. Claus.

Everything was hunky dory until the Latin professor noticed and began quoting Catullus to his tablemates. Their raucous laughter had drawn everyone's attention. A World Religions professor turned puce, and exited the party. The rest of his table followed. JoJo lost it.

Toni grinned as she typed. Across the narrow aisle, Munger gave a great belly laugh and said, "There must be photos."

"Frankie always forgets. But Philo said he'll send his over. There won't be many. He said Frankie was laughing so hard she was choking."

Philo had made their excuses, grabbed a bottle of Prosecco, and half-carried her to his truck. As far as Frankie knew, no one on campus had seen JoJo since that night. Frankie figured she'd been licking her wounds among Florence's marble statuary.

"Apparently not," Toni said, half-aloud.

Munger, notebook and pen in hand, scooted his chair across to Toni's cubicle. Even sitting down, he filled the opening. He'd played rugby in college. Now, training for marathons kept him fit. "But who would have killed her that night?" he said. "Her students?"

Toni had interviewed Frankie while Munger took Philo. She looked at her notes. "Frankie said the three ringleaders were immature, yes, but hardly killers. And they'd appeared properly penitent and anxious as they awaited their punishment—one that never materialized because JoJo had filed their grades before the party, after viewing chaste versions of the centerpiece décor. So, the changes must have been made only minutes before the faculty entered the room."

"Which means the students aren't off the hook."

"Nope. But the fact that Dixon never had a chance to make good on her threat to fail them narrows our timeline." Toni stood, picked up a dry-erase pen, and began adding notes to the line she'd drawn on the white board that served as her cubicle wall. "The murder most likely took place on campus, before she could get back to her office to change the grades."

"If she even planned to make changes," Munger said. "She might have discovered the humor in it belatedly. Or just shrugged off the infractions once she cooled down."

"Maybe. But unlikely."

Toni wrote a question in the white space above the line: Who was JoJo's date that night? Frankie had tried to picture the man with JoJo, but failed. He had been swallowed by the plaster walls, the fluorescent lights, and the clamor of people arriving.

Munger flipped through the pages of his notebook. "First name, Fritz. An engineer. Philo only knew that because Fritz ran into someone he knew at the party—someone he once swam with. But Philo didn't know whether it was a neighborhood swim team or a school team."

"JoJo swam for our high school," Toni said. She picked up her cell and tapped a number from memory. Asked Frankie a couple of questions, then shut off.

"She also swam for Arizona State. Frankie says she was good, not outstanding. But she'd started training again. Frankie wasn't sure where."

Munger wheeled away. "I'm on it."

"Wait." Toni opened an email on her computer. "The autopsy report's back."

They were both silent, reading. Identity: Confirmed. Burial and skull damage: Postmortem. Cause of death: Asphyxiation. Homicide: Confirmed.

"Her hyoid bone was crushed," Toni said.

"So she was choked—or strangled with something. Did you see the note about the recent termination of pregnancy?"

"Yup. We need to get to her dad before the media get ahold of this. Maybe he'll know who the father was."

Munger was already punching buttons. "I'll see if an intern can track down 'Fritz.'"

***

Harley Dixon, M.D., lived in Hidden Valley, northeast of Tucson city limits. Not far from FCC. The Santa Catalina Mountains rose steeply above the neighborhood, named for the Hidden Valley Inn Restaurant. Built to recall Tucson's frontier days, the inn had served BBQ ribs, steak, and prime rib. But it was their display of miniatures that made the restaurant one of Toni's favorite

8

childhood eateries. Before it burned. The rebuilt version lacked the original ambiance.

The neighborhood had been subdivided from a historic ranch. The area had its own, private park with access to Sabino Creek. Toni and Munger turned off on a graveled dirt road that led to the green area bordering the creek. She remembered being awed the first time she visited JoJo's house. Their entire freshman class had gathered there after the funeral mass for JoJo's mother—a subdued affair held on the back patio and around the pool. Dr. Dixon, a cardiac surgeon, had greeted each person at the door. JoJo had been a ghost at his side, her welcoming comments exact echoes of his. Painful for all.

Today, the front gate was open. The Spanish colonial-style house sat toward the front of a sprawling 10-acre suburban ranch. She and Munger got out of their Tahoe and took in the second-story balconies, deep-set windows with desert-brown shutters, and bougainvillea climbing in magenta and apricot waves against the lime-washed walls. The place might have been here since shortly after Hugo O'Connor led Spanish conquistadores to the banks of the Santa Cruz River.

The entire acreage was surrounded by a straw-bale wall, covered with a mud-adobe plaster. Toni, Frankie, and their classmates had helped build the last section of the wall after JoJo's mother succumbed to cancer. They'd planted a lemon tree over her ashes. Today, Toni could smell the tang of rotting lemons overwhelming scents from desert vegetation. But other than the neglected lemon harvest, the house and grounds looked cared for.

A thirty-something woman, wearing work gloves and hat, rounded the corner of the house. She parked her wheelbarrow under the lemon tree and met them on the bottom step below the carved front door. Toni held out her badge so the woman could read it. "We're looking for Harley Dixon. Does he still live at this address?"

"He does." Soft Southern drawl. "But he was called up to Tempe to assist with a surgery. Should be back this evening. I'm Kendra Wallace. Can I help?"

Munger's pen hovered over his notepad. "I'm afraid not. We need to reach Dr. Dixon. The number associated with his vehicle registration doesn't seem to have an answering machine."

Wallace laughed and settled the straw hat more firmly on her head. "He unplugged all the extensions months ago. Hates robocalls."

"Do you have a cell number for him?"

"No cell. He uses a pager. Everything's routed through his scheduler."

"Even calls from his partners?" Toni said.

"Oh, he sold his practice months ago. But he still consults. Hold on. I'll get you the scheduler's number."

She ran up the front steps, pressed a bit of carving in the massive door. An inset door opened in the center of the right side. She stepped out of her Crocs and slipped inside.

Wallace was back in under a minute. A plastic bag dangled from her left hand, still enclosed in work gloves. She glanced at Munger's ringless fingers. He was in his late forties, but looked ten years younger, despite the silver glints in his hair. She handed him the doctor's business card. "My cell number's on the back. And I thought you might want to take some lemons with you. The damn tree produces all year."

"It's not neces—" Toni began.

"Shame to waste them."

"Okay, then." Toni traded her business card for the bulging bag of fruit. "You live here?"

She nodded. "Going on twelve years now. If you're interested in pottery, my studio's in one of the casitas."

Twelve years would make it shortly after JoJo left for university. Toni said, "In case we have trouble reaching Dr. Dixon, would you mind giving me a call when he returns?"

"Happy to."

They got back in their vehicle. The thermometer registered 120 degrees. The monsoon humidity made it feel even hotter. Toni started the engine and Munger set the air conditioner on Lo. They both took swigs from their water bottles.

"I'm betting this place isn't any farther from the recovery site than the school is." Munger was checking the GPS coordinates and the map.

"You're saying JoJo's father or Kendra Wallace killed her?"

"It's possible."

"But if they had, why cart her all the way to the creek? This property is huge. Why not bury her here and plant another lemon tree over her?"

"To distance themselves from the crime?"

"Killers bury victims on their property all the time. But I'll keep an open mind." She sat for a moment, letting the cool air wash over her, then unzipped a daypack she kept on the back seat. Taking out a navy neckerchief, she got out and walked back to where Kendra was half finished with her clean-up under the lemon tree. "Do you have a hose handy?"

"At the corner of the house. Help yourself."

Toni wet the handkerchief, wiped her face, rinsed it again, and tied it around her neck. As she went by Kendra, she said. "Thanks, you're a lifesaver."

"No problem."

Toni nodded at the wheelbarrow "It's a huge property. I'd think you'd have an ATV to haul the trash to the bins—especially in this weather."

Kendra grunted as she dumped another shovelful in the wheelbarrow. "Had one, but it's been out of commission for ages. Harley hasn't gotten around to fixing it yet—or getting a new one."

When Toni was back in the car, she tossed her hat in the back seat, untied the neckerchief and set it on the console. The air in the SUV was down to a tolerable 103 degrees.

"You get another one of your hunches?" Munger said.

She looked in the mirror and began backing up. "I just figured an ATV would be the easiest way to move a body into the wash. Supposedly the doc's has been broken down for a long time."

"Be worth checking."

"But let's not put him on guard just yet. Let's see how he reacts to the news first."

"Meanwhile, we can start making a case for a search

warrant." Munger's phone signaled a text coming through. "An intern figured Ms. Dixon would swim close to where she worked or lived. In this case, it was both. Turns out her swim club uses the campus pool. Fredrick 'Fritz' Stoppard is a member."

"Wait—JoJo was living here?"

"She'd rented out her condo because she was heading off to Italy. Her stuff is probably in one of the casitas Wallace mentioned. And here's the good news—the swim team's due at the campus pool in 10 minutes."

***

The parking lot by the FCC gym was deserted except for a cluster of cars under a trio of mesquites. The outdoor pool was accessed via the gym dressing rooms and a gate in the cyclone fence. Through the fence they could see that all eight swim lanes were occupied.

An attendant checked their badges and wrote their names on his clipboard. He pointed to lane 1, where a male ploughed through the water in an effortless crawl. "Training for the 1500." He nodded toward a tall woman in a red swimsuit walking the edges of the pool. "Coach Lisa Rostov."

Toni and Munger approached Rostov, introduced themselves, and explained what they needed. Rostov was older than she'd appeared from a distance. Late forties. Brown hair tucked up under a wide-brimmed hat. Dark tan. Sunglasses. "This can't wait till Fritz finishes? The meet's next week." She had a faint accent. Slavic, perhaps.

"Sorry, no," Toni said.

Rostov grunted, took a red plastic card from under the roster sheet on her clipboard, and walked to the shallow end. She crouched above lane 1 and waited.

The late afternoon heat and glare were intense. After stopping at the water fountain, Toni and Scott headed for the shaded upper benches of the metal grandstands. From there they watched Rostov slip the card underwater. Stoppard stopped at the wall. Rostov said something and pointed towards the bleachers. He looked up, shrugged, removed cap and earplugs, and hoisted his body out of the pool.

Maybe six-one. Broad shoulders. Tapered torso. Miniscule swimsuit. He towelled off, twisted the water out of the cloth, draped it around his neck, and slid his feet into flip-flops. Slipped on glasses. He knew they were watching, but his movements seemed deliberate, unhurried.

Toni pulled out her cell phone. Took a photo blast. "Does he look like a person that would fade into the woodwork?"

"Maybe with his clothes on."

"The Clark Kent version." She studied Stoppard as he walked toward them. "JoJo was small. Looks like he could have carried her from campus to the creek."

"But like you pointed out at Dixon's house, why transport her? There are acres of private desert here—plenty of places to hide a body."

A conundrum, definitely.

They rose together as Stoppard climbed the bleachers. "Fredrick Stoppard?" Toni showed her ID.

"Call me Fritz." Stoppard shook Toni's hand with his damp one. "Homicide? Who died?"

She told him. The look of surprise on Stoppard's face seemed genuine. "JoJo? But . . . when?"

"The night you escorted her to the campus holiday party."

Stoppard looked confused. "But she was flying to Italy the next morning."

"She was dead long before that."

He sat down with a thunk that rattled the grandstand.

Toni held up her phone. "Do you mind if I record this?"

"No, of course not."

"Tell us about that night, Fritz—everything you can remember."

Stoppard ran a hand through short, sun-bleached hair. "Well, Jojo was seeing someone, but hadn't come out to her department. So I offered to be her plus one."

"Do you know who she was seeing?" Toni said.

"Not by name. But Rostov might. I saw Coach greet the

13

woman once when she came to the pool to pick up JoJo." Anticipating Toni's next question, he said, "About my age. Dark hair. Moved like a dancer. Switch-hitter, I'd say. She looked me over while she waited for JoJo."

"Notice anything else on that occasion?"

"Yeah. She was driving JoJo's car—a red Mercedes."

Munger took out his phone and texted.

"What do you remember about the party?" Toni said.

Fritz ran the towel over his face. "We met at the dining hall. JoJo checked out the centerpieces. I talked to a few people. Can't remember names. I grabbed a beer and went to our table."

"One witness told us that JoJo was upset about the centerpieces."

"I thought they were funny, but JoJo went all Krakatoa. I dragged her outside before she could make a complete ass of herself. Clearly something else was bugging her. I asked her what the deal was. She didn't want to tell me at first, and then she kind of broke down. Said she and her mother caught JoJo's father getting it on with an elf at her family's last Christmas party. Her parents had one hell of a row. Next morning she found her mother floating in the pool. It was ruled a natural death, but JoJo wasn't convinced. Those damn elves brought it all back."

"Did you drive JoJo home?" Toni said.

"No, she had her car. Said she was heading to the airport as soon as she dropped that off and collected her gear. So I left. No word since. Now I know why."

"So you and JoJo parted on friendly terms?"

"Oh, now look—I'd never have hurt JoJo. We've been friends forever."

"Can you think of anyone who might have had a reason to hurt her?"

"Her girlfriend? They had a row before JoJo arrived for the party. I gathered it was because JoJo wouldn't take her along."

"Anyone else?" Scott said.

"Not offhand."

"Okay," Toni said. "We'll need your contact information. And we'll leave our cards with Coach Rostov in case you think of anything else."

Fritz dictated his info to Scott, whose phone buzzed as they followed Stoppard down the bleachers. Scott stopped to talk, then caught up with Toni. "Kendra Wallace says Doctor Dixon should be home within the hour."

Toni checked her watch. They should have time to grab a bite and clean up before the bereavement call.

When they handed their cards to Lisa Rostov, Toni asked if she knew the name of JoJo's partner, the woman Fritz saw driving JoJo's car.

"Kendra Wallace. But she wasn't—"

Toni's cell rang. "Excuse me a minute, Coach."

"This is Harley Dixon." A baritone. Calm. Assured. "You wanted to speak to me?"

Toni introduced herself. "Are you at home, Doctor?" When he said he was, Toni said they'd be there in five minutes.

***

Toni pulled into the driveway. The gate was open, as before. Waiting at the top of the steps was a tall man, sixtyish, with damp silver hair—a grayer version of the man Toni rememberred from the reception after JoJo's mother's funeral and JoJo's high school graduation party. He had his arm around Kendra Wallace. Her left ring finger sported a large diamond engagement ring and matching wedding band. They sparkled in the afternoon light.

"So, Kendra Wallace isn't JoJo's partner," Munger murmured, as they exited the vehicle.

"I wonder what else Stoppard lied to us about?"

As they ascended the steps, Toni fished out her ID and held it up. "Toni Navarro. County Homicide." She gestured to her partner. "Scott Munger."

"Homicide?" An echo of Fritz Stoppard's reaction. Behind the tan, Dixon's skin looked chalky.

"It's pretty hot out here," Toni said. "Could we go inside, please."

15

"Yes, of course."

Dixon led the way into the living room. Kendra had been silent, but once Toni and Dixon were seated, she said, "I'll get us something cold to drink," and left them.

"Is this about about Jo?" Dixon said.

"Yes. I'm sorry. JoJo's remains were found yesterday morning."

He looked at Toni. "You went to high school with my daughter. Are you the one who found her?"

"No, sir. But a classmate of ours did. And she recognized this." Toni showed Dixon the image she'd taken of the gold pin on JoJo's dress.

Dixon glanced at the image, drew in a sharp breath. "Her mother's pin. A high school graduation gift." He settled back into the leather chair, as if drawing strength from its solidity. "Where was she found?"

"Not far from here. In the creek bank."

He nodded. "I knew. Jo wasn't one to write or call, but she never missed my birthday. Or Father's Day. Both were last week." He rubbed his eyes. "You have questions, I suppose. Am I a suspect? Is Kendra?"

"At present we're just gathering information. But your answers might rule you out."

"Then we'd better get started."

"How long have you and Kendra been married?"

"Since Thanksgiving. I sold the practice then, and we spent the next two months touring Australia and New Zealand."

"And Hawaii, going and coming," Kendra added, handing around frosty Arnold Palmers.

Their travels would be easy enough to check. "Then you were out of the country when JoJo was scheduled to leave for Italy."

"Yes," Kendra said. "That trip was her Christmas present from us."

"I have to ask a question—it will be painful."

"What could be more painful than losing your only child?" Dixon said.

Toni gave a little shrug and said, "The autopsy showed that your daughter had terminated a pregnancy shortly before she died. Do you know—"

"Fritz Stoppard," Kendra said. "Jo told me the night it happened. Date rape, but it was a, he said/she said, so she didn't report it. The Italy trip would have given her time to heal."

Toni looked at Scott. He nodded. They had motive and opportunity. Time to put out a BOLO on Stoppard, who was probably halfway to the border. She handed him the Tahoe keys so he could make the call in privacy.

When Scott was gone, Toni said to Dixon, "Another awkward question: Was your daughter gay?"

"Jo?" Kendra laughed. "You've got to be kidding."

Dixon managed a wan smile. "No. But it wouldn't have mattered."

Scott Munger stepped through the front door and sat down. "I noted a surveillance camera over the front door, Doctor. Are there other cameras at the rear? And are they working?"

Dixon nodded. "Our security service archives the feed."

"Do the archives go back eight months?" Munger said.

"They go back two years," Kendra said. "Since he had the system installed."

***

Border police intercepted Fritz Stoppard at the Nogales port-of-entry. He was held there until Toni and Scott picked him up, read him his rights, and arranged for his car to be towed back to Tucson. Once there, criminalists searched and catalogued the contents of the car. It was a gold mine.

While the criminalists were working, Toni and Scott checked the college security tapes and talked to a few of JoJo's students. Five hours later, Toni, Scott, Stoppard, and a public defender sat in an interview room in east Tucson. Munger repeated Stoppard's rights and asked if he understood them. He did.

Toni said, "For the record, Mr. Stoppard, we have established that everything you told us earlier today was a lie."

Silence.

"The evidence contained in your vehicle supports the picture we've constructed of what happened to Josephine Joyce Dixon on the last night of her life." Toni set the first evidence bag, containing a leather-covered journal, on the table between them. "Your journal suggests you were obsessed with Ms. Dixon—had been since you were teenagers."

Munger set another bag on the table. It held a small jeweler's box. Toni tapped the bag. "The night of the Foothills Community College holiday party, you planned to propose to Ms. Dixon."

Munger set a third bag on the table. Stoppard bent his head to his shackled hands, adjusted his glasses, and studied the computer printout. Straightening, his eyes held no expression. "You'd bought a ticket to go with her to Florence," Munger said. "It was a surprise."

"The truth is," Toni said, "you were stalking Ms. Dixon. She hadn't asked you to escort her to the party. You showed up, uninvited. And she was angry. Her students' centerpieces were simply the final straw. When the department chair reacted to her outburst, she retreated to the parking lot. You followed her. She told you she would neither travel with nor marry the man who had raped and impregnated her. And she told you that she'd terminated the pregnancy. Is that summary correct, Mr. Stoppard?"

"No comment."

"You remember those students who made the centerpieces?" Toni said. "They wanted to apologize, so they followed Ms. Dixon to the parking lot. They saw and heard you yell that she had no right to get an abortion without consulting you. They saw her break away from you and drive off. They saw you drive after her. And campus security cameras recorded the same thing."

"You followed her home, Mr. Stoppard. You killed her there, then drove her body to the nearby park. You carried her to the creek and buried her. Do you know how we know this? Because the Dixons also have security. They were out of the country at the time and had never reviewed the archived footage. But those images show your car arriving. They show you carrying JoJo's body and her luggage from her casita to your car. And they show you driving off."

Silence. The lawyer pushed back his chair. "We're finished here."

"She had no right," Stoppard said. Pitiless eyes, fierce tone. " Understand? No right."

~*~

THE GIFT OF CHRISTMAS FUTURE

KRIS NERI

Detective Ariana Vargas of the Tucson Police Department brought her unmarked car to a screeching halt before a house that burglars, in a true bah-humbug act, had hit. The home's decorative Christmas lights flashed in unison with the light bar on the patrol car already parked in its driveway.

Madre de Dios. Could this place get any more festive? Ariana's holiday spirit was always tinged with some sadness, but this year it was trending toward bah-humbug as well. When she stepped from the car, she spotted one of those little evergreen trees the city seemed to be painting on some neighborhood curbs this year.

What were the city officials thinking? Would the green painted trees disappear after the first? Or would they linger all year as a sad reminder of a holiday not everyone appreciated? Ariana felt so frustrated, she longed to kick the tiny painting. Just then a young patrol officer came out from the door of the victims' home. With an angry grunt, Ariana approached him, steeling herself for the bad news.

"Hey, Flynn," she said so tightly her jaw ached.

21

She didn't need to ask if this break-in was like all the others—she could read that in the sympathy on his solemn face. It was another addition to her case, all right. Her unsolved case.

"Hi, Detective. Captain Andrews wants you to report in right now. It just came over the radio," he said.

She knew that. She'd heard the transmission in her own unmarked car. Still, she'd ignore the command as long as possible. She had a good reason for avoiding their superior. Captain Andrews didn't want a report, he wanted an arrest. Something she hadn't been able to deliver in all the weeks of this pre-holiday home robbery crime wave.

"You haven't seen me, Flynn."

The young patrolman smiled, clearly enjoying sharing her secret. "Sure thing, Detective."

That bought her a little time. Tomorrow was her day off. She'd spend all day working this case. Sure, Christmas was only a few days away, and she hadn't finished her shopping. But it wasn't like she had many people in her life to buy gifts for. She also knew the odds of cracking the case in one day were slim. Not when she hadn't turned up a single lead in all the weeks she'd been investigating. Her mood sunk even lower.

"Merry Christmas, Detective," Flynn called, while climbing into the patrol car.

"Yeah, right," Ariana muttered.

Some Christmas. The families the burglars hit weren't going to have good holidays, and neither would she if she couldn't crack this thing. Well, she never really had a great Christmas. By the time she'd started having good holidays, her sour holiday mood had become too embedded for her to completely erase it. Christmas hadn't exactly been a memorable occasion for Ariana. She'd been left at a Tucson firehouse on Christmas Eve when she was only hours old. Even her name was a fiction the social worker assigned to her case had given her before shoving Ariana into a group home until a suitable foster home could be found. Suitable, right.

It was funny, though. She'd spent her whole life in Tucson, where Christmas was always warm and sunny, not cold and

22

snowy. But a small hidden part of her bought into the Christmas card mystique, like everyone else. As a kid, she dreamed that Old White Guy with the beard and red suit would bring her something that would change her life. Not that she ever sat on a mall Santa's knee, or whispered her secret wishes to him—most people wouldn't pay for a foster kid to see Santa. Sure, her luck eventually changed. By the time it did, though, Christmas disappointment was a part of her.

Ariana interviewed the latest burglary victims, an elderly couple from Chicago, who had retired in Tucson. They'd been attracted by Tucson's charm, they told her, the way its diverse population seemed to live in harmony, its warm winters, and its breathtaking desert scenery.

"We hoped Tucson would provide a respite from the big city stresses, such as crime, you know? We wanted a safe place for our grandchildren to visit." The gray-haired older woman had kept most of the accusation from her voice when she said that, but not quite all. Or maybe Ariana simply heard what wasn't there.

Bet they're not feeling so far removed from those stresses now. Tucson's not as big as Chicago. With its wide-open vistas, in the shadow of the Catalina Mountains, for a medium-sized city, it had retained something of a small-town feel. That didn't make it immune from crime, however, as this wave of robberies proved. Even when it truly had been a smaller city, during Ariana's childhood, it never had been crime-free. She had real firsthand knowledge of that.

Ariana heard a familiar story from the victims. Once again, the burglars had been choosy. The burgled homes weren't picked clean. Size, more than value, seemed to govern what was stolen. The thieves took jewelry, handheld electronics, keepsakes, and cash, along with a number of the smaller wrapped packages from under the homeowners' Christmas trees. High-priced TVs, computers, and loads of other valuables—all larger items—were left behind.

This size-business had Ariana baffled. She wondered whether the thief might be a petite woman, but Ariana herself wasn't that large, and she could have carried far bigger items.

When she stepped outside again after the interview, she surveyed the neighborhood. Modest southwestern homes, in a variety of pastel tones, all with neat desert landscaping. Not an affluent street, but solidly middle-class. The kind of neighborhood where people could afford some nice things, but where they'd find it tough to replace them. At this time of the year, the loss of the gifts they'd purchased for their grandchildren would hurt the most. Unfortunately, it also wasn't a neighborhood where people could afford doorbell cameras.

That sort of victimization never ceased to anger Ariana. Even after years of police work, she hadn't become immune to the victims' pain. Perhaps it was a form of making amends since Detective Vargas hadn't always fought on the side of the angels.

While living in a series of abusive foster homes, Ariana had become a confused and angry child, ripe for a manipulative adult to use for his own ends. By the time she was eleven, a man from the neighborhood convinced her to rob houses for him. So needy was she for the praise he bestowed, she never grasped she took all the risks, while that man kept all the gain.

She shuddered to think of where she'd be today if—ironically, only days before an earlier Christmas—Detective Jeffrey Noel hadn't caught her breaking into the home of a friend of his. He carted her back to his own house, kicking and screaming all the way—to the influence of his caring wife, Ruby. White-haired even then, though she wasn't much past fifty, Detective Noel fondly referred to her as Mamá Noel. Mother Christmas, a name that fit with their last name.

Though the Noels had fostered a number of troubled kids over the years, what Jeffrey did that day by bringing her home wasn't legal. But by bending the law, he saved Ariana from what would have been another gloomy Christmas with abusive people. Years later, Jeffrey had insisted he could see the hardness she'd developed hadn't reached much below the surface. He knew she had the potential to become someone better.

On that first day, though, Ariana struggled to seem as jaded as possible. She pretended to find their seasonally decorated house, which Jeffrey dubbed the North Pole, to be lame. Secretly, though, she knew she was about to have the best Christmas since the day of her birth, when she had been left at that firehouse. Despite the melancholy mood that still lingered at this time of the year, every Christmas she'd spent with the Noels had been warm and wonderful.

In the days after that first holiday, Jeffrey followed through with the paperwork. He persuaded the Department of Family Services to place an already-hardened kid into his wife's gentle care. Ariana still secretly referred to what Jeffrey had given her as "the gift of Christmas past." Scrooge didn't have a monopoly on ugly Christmases past.

Ariana's rough edges hadn't been smoothed over in one day, but under those good people's guidance, she gradually left the ways of the street behind her. When it came time to choose her career, she never considered anything other than police work— her tribute to Jeffrey.

Ariana smiled fondly at the thought of Ruby. They would spend the holiday together again in a couple of days, but this time it would be sad for both of them. Jeffrey had passed away last year, and Family Services questioned whether Ruby was too old to foster children anymore. The double-blow was rough on the old woman. Mamá Noel wasn't recovering well. Ariana was scheduled to plead Ruby's case before a Family Services board in January. But a house without kids to share it would make this Christmas awfully quiet.

Before Ariana came to live with the Noels, she couldn't imagine entering a nice neighborhood except to steal. At that time, her foster home had been a rundown mobile home on one of Tucson's roughest streets. Never would she have expected to become a police officer protecting homey neighborhoods like the one she'd visited today. And in her wildest dreams, she would never have envisioned herself becoming a neighbor of the people who lived there. Yet now, her house was only a couple of blocks away from the latest break-in.

Since it was after quitting time, and she was still avoiding Captain Andrews, Ariana went straight home. The Tucson PD let detectives drive their unmarked cars home when they worked late. She stepped from the car, feeling a rush of pride for her little Pueblo-style cottage. Sure, she was behind in the weeding—who would have thought weeds would grow so vigorously in the Arizona desert? But she felt quiet satisfaction for how far she'd come in the world. Honored to be an upstanding part of the city she protected. If only she could feel she was doing a better job of it. Until she cracked this puzzling crime wave, she couldn't share in any part of the holiday's peace.

Ariana noticed a few of those little Christmas trees had been painted on some of her neighborhood's curbs. There was even one in front of her house. That tree hadn't been there when she left that morning. When had the city decided to add those tree paintings to their holiday decorations? She'd seen the usual lights and banners hung downtown and along the various Tucson shopping streets, such as Fourth Avenue and the Lost Barrio, with their art galleries and rustic furniture shops. Strangely, nobody at the PD seemed to know a thing about who was painting those small curbside trees. But if it wasn't the city painting them, who could it be?

She changed into her gardening clothes and set out to attack the weeds, grateful for Tucson's temperate Decembers. The ground was still soft enough to allow her to dig, an activity that always helped her to think. She'd pull weeds until it became too dark.

Apparently, she was not the only one catching up on her gardening. While working in her front yard, one of the town's maintenance vehicles, its truck bed filled with clippings, stopped before her home and trimmed a roadside bush. Ariana watched as they moved from her house to another and cut a second one. Maybe those painted evergreens weren't decorations at all, but a signal to the Maintenance Department of curbside plants in need of attention. Maybe the evergreens weren't meant to be seasonal. Or if they were, they had a dual purpose.

Sure enough, the crew trimmed the roadside trees and shrubs in front of every house where the tiny trees had been painted. Mystery solved.

Well...maybe not. Another question, associated with the

painted trees, occurred to her.

Ariana stripped off her gardening gloves and threw them to the ground. Slowly, she walked to the street to better study those curbside paintings. The green trees in evergreen shapes had clearly been made with a stencil and green spray paint—that alone explained their uniformity. But what about the "ornaments" painted on some of them? She'd noticed a minority of them had also been dabbed with tiny, colorful—albeit crudely drawn—dots that simulated Christmas tree ornaments. A clerk at the PD had even commented on that.

"Those teeny trees are festive," the woman had said, "but the decorations painted on them are the worst. It looks like they hired a bunch of kids to make those ornaments."

"I like them," a police officer insisted. "They suit the season."

Now, while smiling at the memory, another thought hit Ariana. A bunch of kids? Madre de Dios! Was it possible...?

Despite the gardening gear she'd left on the ground, Ariana ran to her unmarked car in the driveway. Her hands trembled with hope when she pulled the key fob from her pocket and pushed the engine start button.

Could I be right? Please, let me be right.

Ariana hastily drove to each of the burgled homes and found that evergreen trees—all with similar decorations—had been painted on the curbs before all the houses that had been robbed. Had the thieves simply co-opted the signal the Maintenance Department meant for its own workers? How was that possible? What if the bad guys didn't choose to rob some of the houses designated for curbside tree trimming?

Another thought scratched at the edge of her mind. Before Ariana gave voice to it, she drove to each of the burgled houses once more, this time not studying the trees themselves, but the ornamentation painted on them.

Could it be...? Sure, it was a code, indicating which houses among those with stenciled trees should be robbed. Maybe they meant: "Nobody home in this house during the day," or "This house doesn't have a dog." Or simply, "Rob this place."

After studying all the primitive decorations, finally, she

understood. Now, she just needed to decide what to do about it.

***

The thieves broke the kitchen window and climbed in over the sink. They snatched the portable CD player on the counter and some small artifacts in the bedroom.

From a darkened closet, Detective Ariana Vargas silently watched the progression of the robbery she'd set up in her own house by painting "ornaments" on the tree on her curb in the same style as the others. After having studied the childishly dabbed decorations on the stenciled trees, she wasn't surprised by the people robbing her house, but she still found it disturbing. The older of the robbers, a girl, might have been all of ten, while the smaller child, a boy, was even younger. No wonder they were limited to the tiniest valuables. Their hands weren't adult-sized, and they were unable to cart away anything heavy.

Ariana let her intruders leave as they had come, before quietly following behind. The little thieves led the unmarked police car watching her house to a van driven by a teenager, who collected the stolen loot. Other unmarked cars would follow the van as the driver made his rounds. Before the night was out, the adult mastermind behind this crime wave would be in custody and most of the kids in the operation would be in Juvenile Hall.

She apprehended her own two thieves as soon as the van was out of sight. She tossed them into the backseat of her car and drove in the direction of the police station on South Stone Street, for what would be the start of a long, but only partially satisfying, night. She might have cracked her case, but a large number of the arrested perpetrators would be children. Too much like her own story for Ariana to stomach.

"You just got lucky, bitch," the older of the kids in her backseat jeered. "You'd a never figured out our deal otherwise."

Dream on, Squirt. Still, while years of police work had made her indifferent to the insults suspects hurled at her, she couldn't ignore them this time. How could anyone be indifferent to young children already so corrupted? Besides, after determining they were foster kids, and not from a particularly good family, she, more than most people, understood how grim their lives had to be for them to make the choices they had.

Suddenly, with no warning to them or herself, Ariana made a U-turn and drove off in another direction.

"Hey, pig," one of the kids said. "This isn't the way to the cop shop or juvie. Where are we going?"

To the North Pole, you lucky little monster. To Mamá Noel's, where'll you'll receive the best gift you'll ever get.

Ariana smiled to herself. As Jeffrey Noel had done years earlier, she was bending the rules to give a couple of troubled youngsters a chance at better lives. She also couldn't imagine a better gift for the woman who had saved her life than to give her a Christmas present of providing a brilliant Christmas Future for two lost kids. Scrooge didn't have a monopoly on great Christmas Futures either.

~*~

THE BIG BANG

MINERVA RAZ

I owe my success in life—debate champion, high school valedictorian, Ivy League college degree, newly launched career in the plummy world of fine arts—to rejecting all my mother's advice. At this moment I'm violating her most repeated maxim. "Stay away from rich people." My mother never learned that rich people are dangerous only if you aren't rich. I'm not rich yet, but what better way to become rich than to curry the favor of the already anointed?

I tap my scarlet fingernails on a clipboard (mani-pedis are de rigueur), waiting as Bunny Henderson, CEO of the Tucson Modernism Society and heiress to a family fortune made from selling cars to generations of Tucsonans, surveys the entrance to the lecture hall where the kickoff for the society's biggest fundraiser of the year is poised to begin. I'm the Director of PR, but waiting for, or waiting on, Bunny sums up most of my daily activities. I remind myself for the thousandth time this job is a step in my career. One more year and I'll apply for a museum PR job. MOMA, Whitney, Guggenheim.

"Emma, my PR whiz kid, I expected better from you." Bunny gestures at the creased white banner with black lettering hanging over the lecture hall door. "Tucson Modernism Festival Kickoff." Ash blond hair falls in waves around her face. Her lips, cheeks, and forehead are strategically plumped from monthly Botox injections. Tangerine-colored octagons blaze on her vintage Halston wrap dress. "We've had this banner for years. I asked you to design a new one."

I swallow a retort about the entire event showing its age. "Phillip told me we don't have the budget for a new banner." Phillip is the CFO of the Tucson Modernism Society, an impressive title if you ignore that there are only four full-time staff members.

At the sound of Phillip's name, Bunny coos. "Silly boy. We have plenty of money. Leslie gave us a generous donation a month ago."

I roll my eyes. "Not that generous. She refused to fund the social media campaign featuring her vintage Caddy collection." I worked hard designing the campaign. Shots with vintage cars overlaid on pictures of Speedway, Tucson's main drag, from the 1950s, interspersed with photos of young people on the town, then and now.

Bunny shrugs. "Leslie's a bitch. On the first day of kindergarten, she tripped me at recess so she could beat me to the swings. It's a miracle we're still friends."

"Where is Leslie?" I ask. "We need to start the rehearsal."

"Who knows? I'll start without her." Bunny extends one hand out in front of her. "Prepare to be lulled to sleep by our keynote speaker who will titillate your imagination with her latest research on mitered corners in Tom Gish's early doorways."

Why is Bunny being difficult? "Our regulars love Dr. Perkins. The kickoff dinner is almost sold out."

Bunny purses her lips, revealing creases at the edges of her mouth. "Palm Springs modernism events sell out within an hour. What makes them special?"

"Hollywood celebrities, wild parties, famous architects," I pause, lifting a penciled eyebrow.

Bunny waves dismissively. "Everyone thinks Tucson is a sleepy Spanish pueblo. We have more mid-century modern houses than Palm Springs." Gold bangles curve elegantly around her sun-wrinkled arm and settle into each other as if they were designed to be a single bracelet.

"New bracelets?" I ask.

Bunny caresses the gold rounds. "Tiffany. A gift from Phillip. He gave Leslie a matching set."

"My bracelet is Tiffany too." A single circle of interlocking silver chain links graces the smooth skin on my arm. I found the bracelet in the soap dish of the dorm shower during my first year of college. A pale shadow of Bunny's gold. Desire flashes through me in a burst of heat. Patience. I must be patient. I want to ask how Phillip can afford gold Tiffany bracelets on his nonprofit salary but decide not to be catty. "We need to start rehearsing. It's 3:30."

Bunny flings her head back, one hand lifting towards her forehead like a dying swan from a ballet. "Let's start this festival off with a bang. A big bang."

As if summoned by Bunny's request, a bang rings through the courtyard. Bunny drops her hand.

"Do you think—" she begins.

"That was a gunshot," I finish.

Bunny takes off towards the lecture hall doors faster than a sexagenarian in four-inch platforms should be able to move.

Shouldn't we be running for cover? I slide towards the door, peering inside.

A blonde-haired woman in an orange-patterned dress identical to Bunny's slumps face-down over the podium. Scarlet drops of blood drip off one white hand onto the floor.

If Bunny weren't standing in the aisle, I would have sworn the body was hers. Is this a PR stunt?

"Leslie!" Bunny's scream echoes in the empty auditorium.

Marta, Bunny's second-in-command, runs onto the stage from behind the curtains. "I was in the courtyard when I heard a shot. Saw someone running away, but I couldn't see their face." Marta pulls a phone out of her Ralph Lauren tailored navy suit jacket. She speaks, voice muffled. I hear scraps of words. "Shooting. One person. Shooter at large." Marta slips the phone back into her pocket. "Paramedics and police are on the way."

Bunny hops onto the stage. "Is she alive?"

Marta approaches the body. "Doesn't look good."

"Emma and I were out front. We didn't see anyone," Bunny

said.

I step into the auditorium, hovering near the door. I can't shake the fear the killer is among us. Dying on the job is not part of the bargain. No one else seems concerned.

"Bunny. Darling." Philip skids across the stage, dressed in a navy-blue linen jacket and white slacks. Despite the forward motion, his coiffed blond hair stays firmly in place.

"Someone shot Leslie." Bunny flings herself into Phillip's arms, deep sobs shuddering through her body.

"Why do you think it's Leslie?" I ask.

Phillip answers. "Leslie bought a dress to match Bunny's. Matching dresses are so MCM."

Bunny's head pops up, mascara and eyeliner intact despite the racking sobs. "Why would anyone want to kill Leslie? And right before our kickoff event. We're ruined."

Phillip pats Bunny's shoulder. "Maybe the killer didn't mean to kill Leslie."

"You don't mean, you can't possibly think, oh my god." Bunny's hand drapes back over her forehead. "I feel faint."

Marta pushes a chair towards Bunny. Phillip lowers Bunny into the chair, her head slumps over, shoulders heaving.

I wait for actors dressed in 1960s attire to troop in, each with a motive to kill. Is a murder mystery dinner Bunny's idea of a big bang?

Sirens wail outside, then stop. I hear doors slam. Two uniformed paramedics race up the aisle.

One of the paramedics looks at Bunny. "Is she okay?"

Bunny groans.

"She's fine." Marta points at Leslie. If it is Leslie. "She's not."

The paramedics poke around for a minute or two, then back away from the body. The older one shakes his head. "She's a goner."

Two uniformed police officers appear. "Everyone away from the body," one officer barks. If this is a PR stunt, the attention to detail is admirable.

A hand grabs my shoulder and shoves me out of the aisle.

"Detective Morales here." A tall thin man in a grey suit with sleeves that ride above his wrists strides down the aisle towards the podium. "Who found the body?"

Marta raises her hand. I catch a glint of gold bangles that match Bunny's. Why did Phillip give Marta bracelets? More importantly, where is my set?

"I'll talk to you first." The detective spins around. "The rest of you need to leave."

Bunny stands up. In her four-inch platforms, she towers over the detective. "The kickoff event for the annual Tucson Modernism Society fundraiser starts in three hours. In this lecture hall. I'm not leaving."

Marta chokes. She clasps her hand over her mouth, but I can hear her laughter.

Detective Morales frowns. "This is a murder investigation. I can't have anyone tampering with the evidence."

"Murder," Bunny sways.

Phillip wraps his arm around her waist. "Why murder?"

The detective rolls his eyes. "We have a woman dead by a gunshot wound to the temple. No gun in sight. How would you interpret those facts?"

Bunny isn't big on facts, but she is devoted to her festival. A heated argument ensues. In the end, a call from Bunny's father, the esteemed Stan Henderson whose smiling face graces half the billboards in town, results in a compromise. The police cordon off the lecture hall. Officers fan out into the surrounding neighborhood in search of the mysterious intruder. The event will proceed in the garden where tables are already set up for dinner.

A television station van arrives as we leave the lecture hall. Time for the PR whiz kid to shine. I pull out my phone for a few quick tweets before the camera crew reaches me.

After the camera crew leaves, we gather in the courtyard to arrange flowers and set out society literature.

Detective Morales pokes his head out of the back door of the stage at intervals, calling each of our names for interviews. Mine is last. He probably thinks I know nothing. The detective has shed his coat. Yellow circles of past sweat marks haunt the armpits of his white shirt. He is right. I know nothing. Neither does he, as far as I can tell. The mystery perpetrator has vanished. Almost as if they never existed.

The dinner is packed. Nothing like a cold-blooded murder to attract attention. I stand at the edge of the courtyard listening to Bunny offer a rambling tribute to Leslie's dedication to mid-century culture, her steadfast support of the society, and her undying friendship. Bunny dabs a tissue at the corner of her eye, bangles clinking.

I hear more bangles clinking as Marta appears out of the shadows. Her long dark hair is pulled back into a carefully worked chignon at the nape of her neck. I can't ever remember seeing Marta with a hair out of place.

"Bunny's a great actress," Marta whispers. "You'd never know she and Leslie were arguing earlier."

"About what?" I love information.

"I heard angry voices and went to investigate. Leslie told Bunny she was an old fool." Marta pauses as Bunny finishes her speech with an outpouring of gratitude for the support of her audience. "I think Leslie was threatening to pull funding."

"We'd never make it without Leslie's support." I stop. "But I suppose we'll have no choice now."

"Not to worry. Leslie set up a perpetual grant for the society through her foundation. Now that she's passed, we're safe." Marta reaches out to pat my arm. Gold bangles glint in the dim light.

"Bunny said Phillip bought matching bracelets for her and Leslie. Did he buy you a set?"

Marta caresses the bracelets. "Leslie gave me hers. Said she wouldn't accept them."

"Does Phillip know?"

Marta shrugs. "Who cares?"

From the podium, Bunny introduces her loyal assistant Marta, with the society for an astonishing fifteen years. Marta leaves the shadows and walks up to the stage amid polite clapping. Fifteen years waiting for Bunny's job. Marta will be waiting for at least fifteen more at the rate Bunny's going. No way am I making that mistake.

I feel a hand on my arm.

Phillip's cologne gives him away. "Darling, I have a proposition."

I whirl around. "I thought I made myself clear." Phillip propositioned me my first week on the job. After my cutting refusal, I don't know why he'd try again.

Phillip's face, half in the shadows, twitches. "Not that kind of proposition."

I raise an eyebrow.

"I've noticed how observant you are. As am I. If we team up, we can solve this mystery before the police have a clue."

"Why should we care?" Does Phillip think someone we know killed Leslie?

Phillip leans toward me. "Do you care about your job?"

I nod, taking a step back. Phillip knows I need this job. As does he. And Marta.

Phillip continues. "Who, or should I say what, is the main beneficiary of Leslie's will?"

I don't know, but based on Marta's assurances I'm willing to guess. "The society?"

Phillips nods. "And who is the society? You're smart enough to see where I'm heading. The police won't be far behind. They like to keep things simple."

Is Phillip implying that Bunny killed Leslie? "Bunny was with me when the shot was fired."

Phillip sighs. "Rich girls like Bunny hire out their dirty work."

I remember Bunny's odd behavior earlier. The perfect timing of the shot.

At the podium, Dr. Perkins accepts the microphone. The crowd settles, lulled by the drone of her voice. From across the courtyard, I glimpse a blue uniform. "What's in it for me?"

"Your job. Bunny's undying gratitude."

The gold bangles flash in my mind. "Not enough. If we solve this crime, I want a set of the gold Tiffany bangles."

Phillip shifts his weight. "Such a material girl."

I hold out my hand. "Shake on it?"

Phillip's hand is warm and sweaty. I resist the urge to wipe my hand on my dress. "Did you know that Marta overheard Leslie and Bunny arguing? Leslie was threatening to pull funding."

"Marta told you that?" I observe the note of surprise in his voice. Real or fake? Hard to tell.

I nod. "And she has Leslie's bangles. Claims Leslie gave them to her."

The choking noise emanating from Phillip is undeniably real. He spins and walks into the darkness.

***

The death of a local socialite is the headline in the morning news. My murder mystery dinner theory evaporates. From the article, I learn the police found a gun in a hedge down the street from the lecture hall. No fingerprints. It's a ghost gun, so no serial number. The police will run tests, but likely the gun is the murder weapon.

Phillip and I meet for breakfast at the mid-century modern diner that sponsors all our events. Ostensibly we are reviewing plans for the festival.

Phillip pulls out a black leather notebook. Opens to a clean white page. "Let's start with a list of suspects."

I take note of Phillip's trimmed nails with a light buff of clear polish. I'm not the only one spending my hard-earned cash on manicures. Phillip pronounces each name as the page fills. "Bunny. Burglar. Jilted boyfriend. Hired hit man."

I sip dark black coffee in a thick white mug, feeling like Agent Cooper, but without supernatural assistance. Glancing around the diner, I spy Marta at another booth, leaning towards an older lady in a flowered sundress that I would expect to see on a twelve-year-old at a garden party. Diane. One of our board members. Some rich people aren't worth emulating.

"Marta's here." I offer.

Phillip glances up. "I know." He continues writing. "Marta. Phillip. Emma."

"Wait a minute." I clunk the mug down on the laminate tabletop. "How would I have killed Leslie? I was with Bunny. I

38

don't have the money to hire a hit man."

Phillip shrugs. "Just covering our bases."

I can't see how we're making progress. "What jilted boyfriend? Leslie hasn't had a boyfriend in living memory. And if it was a burglar, why wasn't anything taken?"

Phillip scowls. "Someone took Leslie's bangles."

I snort. "Do you seriously think Marta would kill for a set of bangles?"

Phillip looks up from his list. "Not just for the bangles."

I shift my gaze back to Marta, watching as she leans towards Diane. Maybe Marta doesn't want to wait another fifteen years. "And you?"

Phillip smiles. "Everyone knows how close I am to Bunny. Maybe I'm her hired hand."

No doubt he expects me to laugh, but I refuse to give him the satisfaction.

***

I start my investigation at our Danish mid-century modern furniture exhibition that evening. Dan, a white-haired board member, stands alone running his hand over the polished top of a teak buffet. I sidle over.

"Lovely piece," I comment.

Dan looks at me, eyes running down my body. "Lovely indeed."

Time to redirect the conversation. "Such a tragedy about Leslie."

Dan shakes his head. "Leslie. Always trouble."

I gaze up with an encouraging smile.

He clears his throat. "No point speaking ill of the dead, but Leslie knew how to focus on people's weak points, turn the knife in the wound."

I nod, thinking of the time Leslie leaned over and whispered "H&M" in my ear, tugging on the armhole of my favorite little black dress.

"Anyone angry enough to kill her?" I ask.

Dan shrugs. "Everyone she knows has probably wanted to kill her at some point. Could even be someone in this room."

I hear Bunny calling my name. I catch sight of her across the room, frantically waving. She is wearing another Halston dress tonight, this one decorated with swirling patterns of psychedelic pink and green. Excusing myself, I make my way over.

"Have you seen Marta? Or Phillip?" The gold bangles clink softly on Bunny's wrist.

I pause to think. "I saw them at the opening of the reception. I haven't seen them since."

Bunny frowns as she scans the crowd.

"Good turnout tonight," I offer. "We're receiving great publicity."

"I suppose that's a blessing." Bunny turns to look at me. "Find Marta or Phillip for me."

"Can't you call them?" I'm itching to corner another board member.

"I've been calling for the past fifteen minutes. No answer. I'm counting on you." Bunny's green eyes drill into me.

I visualize Phillip and Marta at the door earlier, both dressed in cream linen suits. It will be hard to find them in the crowd. After wandering around for a few minutes, squeezing past guests admiring teak chairs and sleek chrome-and-glass tables, I run into Marie, another board member, clad in a black A-line dress with stylized white flowers that looks straight out of Marlo Thomas's wardrobe for That Girl.

"Love your outfit. Is the dress vintage?" Rich women always want to talk about their clothes.

Marie smiles, cheeks wrinkling. Will a facelift be in order soon? "Mary Quant. Belonged to my mother." She spins around, the dress billowing. Facing me, she sighs. "Great turnout, but I can't help but feel guilty about poor Leslie."

"Why should you feel guilty?" I ask.

Marie leans towards me. Drops her voice. "Leslie wanted the board to hire an auditor. She suspected financial irregularities."

I widen my eyes. "Do you think Leslie's death had something

to do with the society?"

Marie frowns. "Why else would someone kill her?"

Time to try Phillip's theory. "Bunny was wearing the same dress as Leslie. Do you think she was the intended victim?"

Marie laughs. "Bunny loves to hog the spotlight. If someone wanted to kill her, they would have done it."

I look up and see Bunny glaring at me from across the room. Time to move on. I dodge around a barrier into the back work area. Marta's voice carries through a closed office door. "Do you think she suspects anything?"

The reply is too muffled to make out the words. Smooching noises follow.

I understand why Bunny is frantically searching. Time to break up the party. "Phillip. Marta. Are you here? Bunny's looking for you."

The smooching noise stops. Phillip calls out. "Be there in a minute. Just checking some invoices." A minute later Phillip opens the office door, blond hair coiffed, linen suit crisp. He pulls the door closed behind him.

"Is Marta with you?" I ask.

Phillip shakes his head. "No idea where she might be." He places his hand on my back and guides me towards the gallery. "Keep an eye on Marta. She's the only one who witnessed the fight between Leslie and Bunny. And the only one who saw the mysterious intruder."

***

Later that evening, perched on the bed in my studio apartment, I make notes on my findings.

•Phillip and Marta are having an affair. Bunny suspects.

•Fight between Bunny and Leslie. Did it happen, or did Marta make it up?

•Was there an intruder?

•Leslie suspected financial irregularities. Is Phillip embezzling? Or is he protecting someone else?

•Was Bunny the intended victim?
I circle Marta's name. Then Phillip's. My primary suspects.

***

Phillip insists on meeting at the diner the next morning. This evening is our Malibu Beach House event, a formal dress reception with bottomless Manhattans and circulating waiters holding trays of bacon-wrapped dates and pimento-stuffed olives. The house is in Tucson, not Malibu, on a golf course and not a beach, but it could be straight out of Malibu with a two-story living room with floor-to-ceiling windows and a rock wall dominated by a double-sided fireplace. Bunny recently finished a two-year renovation, restoring the house to mid-century perfection. The reception is the only event that sold out immediately. I'm impatient to start work at Bunny's house, but I agree to meet. Maybe I can learn more from Phillip than he intends to tell me.

As soon as I sit down, Phillip leans over the table and asks what I've discovered.

"I talked to several board members. They thought Leslie discovered something."

Phillip raises an eyebrow. "About what?"

"The society."

Phillip snorts. "Doesn't narrow things down much." He pulls out his list.

"Makes it less likely the killing was random. Or unrelated."

"Not good for Bunny. Remember our goal." Phillip writes "Mistaken Identity" in large letters. Taps his pen on the words.

"I mentioned that theory to Marie. She thought it was unlikely."

Phillip snorted. "What do any of those board members know? Don't waste your time talking to them." He reaches for my wrist. Caresses my Tiffany bracelet. "Interesting that you can afford Tiffany on your meager salary."

I jerk my wrist away. "A gift from a friend."

He lifts an eyebrow. "The police may be asking."

42

I stare at Phillip. I didn't expect this game.

Phillip stands. "We all need to watch our backs." He turns to leave, then turns back. "I hear the police will be at the event tonight."

***

At 5:45 pm a line of cars stretches down Bunny's driveway. Bunny and I stand in the foyer at the top of the cantilevered staircase.

The caterers are laying out trays of food on the dining room buffet.

Storyboards on wooden easels show the before pictures, 1980s-era mirrored walls, brassy chandeliers, and white tile floors, all stripped away in the renovation. The original polished terrazzo floor and teak paneling were restored. Reproduction starburst light fixtures were added to match the period. Similar storyboards appear in all the rooms. My handiwork.

Bunny pokes her finger at the nearest board. "Do you think people will appreciate what I've done to the house?"

"The remodel is historically sensitive. And stunning. What's not to like?" I'm always surprised that rich people care what anyone thinks. When I have as much money as Bunny, I won't care.

I peer into the courtyard below. Men in tuxes and women in long sleek dresses accented with sparkling jewels exit from Mercedes and Porsches. Bunny is wearing a vintage blue silk Balenciaga with a sequined belt. The omnipresent gold bangles clink on her wrist. I'm sporting a red silk Halston gown that blouses around my waist and falls in pleats to the floor. Bunny pulled it out of her closet earlier when I appeared in my usual black sheath.

Marta, dressed in her navy suit, hovers over the caterers.

Bunny leans towards me. "Don't you think it's peculiar how Marta arrived at the crime scene so quickly? Conveniently saw the mysterious figure run away?"

I assume she doesn't expect me to answer. I remember

43

Phillip's admonition last night. All roads lead to Marta.

Marta turns and sniffs at my outfit. "Borrowed?"

"Jealousy doesn't suit you." Bunny pulls a key out of her evening bag. "Emma, be a darling and lock up my bedroom."

I take the key and head down the hall. Marta comes up behind me. "Don't think you're special."

I tap the bangles on her wrist. "Phillip thinks you stole those from Leslie."

Marta grabs my arm. "Leslie suspected Phillip of embezzlement."

I yank my arm away and head into Bunny's bedroom, shutting the door behind me. The floor-to-ceiling windows on this side of the house look down over the garden with the glowing blue pool and brightly lit bar. I stand by the window, imagining what it must be like to wake up every morning with the view of the emerald grass of the golf course and the blue sky beyond. Hearing a noise, I peek into the office connected to the bedroom. Phillip stands in front of a desk holding a piece of paper. He looks up as I enter.

"Emma. I didn't expect to see you here."

"Bunny asked me to lock up."

Phillip drops the paper into a drawer and motions toward the door. I'm dying to know what's on the paper, but Phillip hovers in the hall as we exit, watching me turn the key in the lock and slip it into my evening bag.

Marta and I stand in the foyer welcoming guests. As Phillip predicted, Detective Morales appears in a baggy black suit. He places his finger against his lips and disappears into the crowd.

After all the guests have arrived, I peer into the living room. Bunny is holding court by the fireplace, describing the acid washing process that revitalized the lava rock wall.

Guests murmur in admiration as they swill Manhattans.

Marta and Phillip are nowhere in sight.

I duck into the hallway and slide the key into the bedroom lock. The sun is setting. I can barely see, but I leave the lights off to avoid attracting attention from the partygoers at the bar below. I slide the paper out of the desk drawer. An invoice from Tiffany & Co. for two sets of gold bangles. Addressed to the society. Not

Phillip. Did Phillip plant the invoice to implicate Bunny? I fold the invoice and tuck it into my evening bag.

"Not so fast, darling."

I whirl around. Phillip stands in the doorway.

"Such a shame. We made a good team." He walks towards me.

Fear arrives in a paralyzing rush. I push it away. Scope out options for escape. The office has only one door. The one blocked by Phillip. "I'm happy to stay in for my set of bangles."

Phillip advances. I press myself against the window next to a floor lamp. "I'm afraid that won't be possible." I smell the vermouth on his breath.

Phillip pulls a pearl-handled pistol out of his pocket. Not as pretty in person as they sound on the pages of a Raymond Chandler novel.

"I'm afraid your remorse over the embezzlement has led you to suicide."

"Embezzlement?" I ask.

Phillip's look is full of pity. "The Tiffany bracelet. New clothes. New car."

The pity makes me angry. But I can't afford anger. I need to distract him. "You and Marta planned the murder."

Phillip smiled. "Leslie was on to us. We needed to get rid of her."

"Bunny is on to you, too."

Phillip bursts into laughter. "Darling, you are so naïve. Bunny is the mastermind behind our scheme."

I imagine my blood splattering on the window. A spectacle for our guests. Glancing down, I see Marta in conversation with Detective Morales near the bar. I hatch a plan. Risky, but the pistol gives me no choice.

"Please give me another chance." I launch myself into Phillip's arms. Plant my mouth on his. Step on the lamp switch. Kick the window hard. I glance down and see Marta's mouth gape in astonishment. The gun drops to the carpet.

"You're crazy." Phillip pushes me away.

I kick the gun, but it doesn't go far.

Phillip dives onto the carpet one hand reaching for the gun.

I stomp on his arm, but Phillip is strong. I can't keep him down.

Salvation appears in the form of Marta, bursting through the door, face twisted into a knot. "Cheating liar," she screams as she flings herself onto Phillip's back, pummeling him with her fists.

I kick the gun again. It lands in the doorway, at the feet of Detective Morales.

"Party's over." Detective Morales points his gun at Phillip and Marta. They freeze.

"Stupid bitch," Phillip hisses. "You ruined everything."

I'm not sure if Phillip is talking to Marta or me.

I watch the police handcuff Phillip and Marta and herd them out of the room. Now that I'm safe, I start to shake.

Bunny rushes in and helps me to a chair. "I knew I could count on you," she says.

***

Two days later Bunny and I meet at the diner for breakfast. Bunny reaches over the table and grasps my hand. "I have the most wonderful news. The board met last night and appointed you vice president of the society."

"I'm honored." I caress the gold bangles on my arm. Bunny's gift. She couldn't stand to wear them after Phillip's betrayal.

The police are holding Marta's set as evidence.

Marta and Phillip insist that Bunny was part of the plan to kill Leslie, but no one believes them.

The police have uncovered no evidence. Detective Morales questioned me yesterday for an hour.

Bunny picks up her coffee cup. "Emma darling. What did you tell the police?"

I pick up my cup. "You were with me at the time of the shooting. That's all I know."

Bunny smiles. "We're going to be a wonderful team."

I clink my cup against hers. "To the future of the society."

I think of the Tiffany invoice tucked into a random novel on my bookshelf. Bunny has no idea what a wonderful team player I can be.

~*~

THE DEVIL IS IN THE DETAILS

MARY BALL

My hand shakes as I lift my garden hose to spray my bougainvillea. My beloved flowers need relief from the heat and the dry desert air. I pray we have a wet monsoon season this year; the whole Southwest suffers from a long, drawn-out drought. I live on a golf course in the Catalina foothills in Tucson, and the greens have been looking sickly for a couple of years now.

And there's the flack we get from the environmentalists. They have a point, but Jack and I saved for years to move to our beloved retirement community with palm trees, winding golf cart trails, pools, a community center, and a clubhouse. Sunset years in paradise, that's the promise we cling to. But no one mentioned we'd would still be the same old people we were before retirement, with the same old baggage. And we have plenty of baggage. And that is the trouble. Paradise in Tucson did not solve our problems.

I sigh; it's going to be a long day. The sun is just coming up, and the Santa Catalinas are glowing in the magic light of sunrise as the world turns gold and glorious. Arizona isn't on daylight savings, so the summer sunrise is pretty early. It's five-thirty, but I couldn't sleep. I've got a busy day ahead of me.

***

And the day drags on; time can crawl when you need to get something over with. I recheck my watch, it's nearly one o'clock. My morning was more difficult than I dreamed it would be. "The Devil is in the details." I remember that saying, and I keep getting the details wrong this morning. It almost spoiled the rest of my day.

I consider tidying the house because we expect the Reverend Johnson today, but I can't concentrate. Nerves, I guess.

I step outside to check my pool. The water sparkles blue and inviting in the bright sun. Something about the sight of water is calming; I am desperate to remain calm. I turn my patio fan to high and try to meditate.

The reverend will be here soon. Everything is ready—a pot of tea, his favorite cookies, and the desk in the study is cleared of clutter where the reverend and Jack prefer to work. Jack's accounting skills come in handy for the church. The church board might think about paying him. I shrug. That won't happen.

I'll practice my yoga until the reverend arrives. Jack won't mind. I sit back in lotus position, take a deep breath, and let it out slowly to calm myself.

"You-hoo, Carrie." My brief attempt at calm is interrupted by Molly Mason. You should be so lucky to have Molly as a next-door neighbor. Seriously, I'd be glad to give her to you. Molly knows everything about everyone on the street, and I'm about to be bombarded with news of what poor Mr. Smith learned at the oncologist yesterday and what time Tim Akins snuck home last night. I know Molly will clutch her hands to her heart and mummer over the suffering of both Mr. Smith and Tim's wife.

I'm not in the mood for her right now, but it would be easier to halt a hurricane than stop Molly from unlatching the gate between our two houses and bustling onto my patio. The slam of the gate shortens my next deep breath. I squeeze my hands together to halt their shaking, plaster what I hope is a smile, not a grimace, on my face, and turn to face The News Hour with Molly Mason.

"What a beautiful day," Molly always starts with the weather report, "It's supposed to rain tonight."

"We sure could use a good drenching." I make the expected response.

The mundane over, Molly jumps right into the lead story. "They took Mr. Smith to the hospital last night. Did you hear the ambulance?"

Last night Jack and I were in an overheated discussion. I didn't hear anything except his rant. When I don't respond in three seconds, Molly continues her monologue. "I don't think he'll be returning from this one." Molly has the strange ability to look appropriately grave and still convey that high excitement of imparting news.

"It might be a blessing; the poor man is suffering." I borrow this line from another of Molly's monologues. She won't recognize it as her own—it's too sappy.

I give up on meditating and offer Molly a glass of iced tea. I serve it on the patio even as the temperature hovers near 100 degrees; the fan will keep us cool enough. I don't invite Molly into the house. She'd give a home inspection report during her nightly news to the rest of the neighborhood, and for once, they would listen.

But now I learn that Tim arrived earlier than usual last night, around ten, and he didn't appear drunk. I'm happy for his wife.

"Your flowers are prettier than last year." Molly takes a moment to smell the roses. Then she gets down to the brass tacks of her visit. "I noticed you drove off three times this morning and returned with sacks from the Safeway. Did you lose your shopping list?"

It was that jar of pickles. The Devil is in the details, and I screwed up this morning, big time. Jack wanted a ham and cheese sandwich, potato chips, and sweet gherkins for lunch. I wrote out my shopping list and promised him I'd be back to fix his lunch in a half-hour. And as promised, a half-hour later, I made his sandwich the way he likes it, toasted whole wheat, a liberal spread of real mayonnaise, and a leaf of lettuce soaked in ice water to crisp it. Next, his favorite deli ham sliced thick, followed by sharp cheddar cheese. I slice the sandwich diagonally. I once cut it straight, and he threw the plate at me. I rarely make the same mistake twice with Jack. Next, I drained three sweet gherkins and placed them neatly on his plate before adding exactly two handfuls of chips.

Jack was sitting in the study watching the "World Federation of Wrestling" on cable. I placed his lunch and a twist-capped Bud on the table beside his recliner. "Thanks," he grunted, his eyes never leaving the TV. He took a bite of the pickle, spit it out, stood up, and threw the plate at the wall. "You ignorant bitch," he shouted at me. "These are not Nancy's Fancy Gherkins."

The sandwich fell apart against my spring-blue wall. A line of mayo traced the path of the bread as it slid to the floor. Chips flew around and settled on the carpet. I scurried about, picking up the mess while apologizing to my husband.

"I'm so sorry, Jack." I kept my head down, not meeting the fury in his eyes. "These pickles were on sale, I was trying to save you money."

Jack regularly goes through my bills and complains about the cost of my favorite treats. He never complains about the cost of his beer.

"I'll be back in a jiffy with the ones you want," I promised.

"You damn well better be. I'm hungry, and the reverend will be here any time now." He settled back to watch his show. His entire reprimand took place during a commercial break. Lucky for him, he missed none of the action.

***

I close my eyes and take a deep breath, trying to think of something to say to Molly, who is watching me for reactions. I shrug. "I had a little problem getting Jack's lunch right."

It's not that Molly doesn't know about Jack. She has heard the shouting and caught me in a moment of weakness, crying on my patio. She knows my bruises aren't from running into walls. Still, we keep up the pretense.

"You're a saint, putting up with that man," Molly says. I don't know if she is genuinely kind or fishing for details for her next exclusive.

"It was nothing, my mistake."

Nothing? I think back on my morning. I can't believe what I did next. I wanted this day to be perfect, and I made such a dumb mistake. I had rushed back to the store, breaking the speed limit and failing to come to a full and complete stop before turning into Safeway's parking lot. I grabbed a jar of Nancy's Fancy Gherkins and rushed back home. Once more, I toasted his bread, spread the mayo extra thick, and added the ham and cheese. I placed the pickles in an artistic display, and then I double-checked the label.

I slammed my hand against my forehead. How could I have been so stupid? These are Nancy's Fancy DILL Gherkins. My entire body trembled as I imagined Jack's reaction if I had offered them to him. I was shaking, but I lucked out. He was so busy with that wrestling show, shouting encouragement to his favorite and hollering obscenities at the referee that he hadn't heard me come in. He had drained the bottle of Bud I gave him and helped himself to another one. I grabbed my car keys and slipped out the back door.

***

I'm shivering, remembering the incident.

"You seem a little nervous today." Molly comments.

"Too much caffeine," I tell her. "My doctor is trying to get me to cut back." I don't know when I became such a quick and smooth liar. That's a lie. I know exactly when I told my first "what happened to you?" story. It was three months after I married Jack. Our honeymoon ended abruptly. I had forgotten to put gas in his car, and he was in a hurry to meet up with his hunting buddies. He poured a long angry burst of obscenities and then slapped me so hard I nearly passed out. I stumbled away from him, sobbing.

And then, as quickly as it had come, his anger was gone. "Carrie, I'm so sorry. I didn't mean to hit you." He hugged me, crying with me. "It will never happen again, I swear."

53

And I believed him.

It wasn't a year later that he hit me again. This time leaving half of my face black and blue, and that's when I came up with the "walking into walls" excuse. But he was so sorry. The second time he bought me an emerald ring and took me to Vegas. We had a great time, and he promised to get help with anger management when we returned home.

And I believed him.

It wasn't until the third incident and long-drawn-out apology that I quit believing him.

Why did I stay? For years the good times far outnumbered those sudden outbursts of anger. I would be apprehensive for a month or two and then relax, convincing myself he had gotten better. In the last few years, I've come to understand, he is never going to get better. But where could I go? He controls all of our money.

***

I shake my head. Those pickles rattled me. Here I am reminiscing over my entire marriage while the sharp-eyed Molly studies me. I had better be careful. Anyway, I tell her, "I managed to make his lunch perfectly, and he's thrilled."

Well, he was pleased. I'm not sure how he felt after lunch. I didn't check.

I had rushed to the store one more time. Peter Simpson, Tucson PD, stopped me. "Where's the fire, Carrie?" he asked.

Peter is a friend but not the most imaginative cop in the world. "Sorry, I'm late getting Jack's lunch."

Peter nodded. He knew about Jack and understood why I was wringing my hands. "Be careful." He let me go with that brief warning.

I returned home from the grocery store. I had read the label three times before buying, remembering to remain calm and check the details: Nancy's Fancy Sweet Gherkins. Once more, I made his sandwich perfectly, arranged the pickles on his plate, and added the chips.

I counted the empty bottles of Bud—four—as I carried his lunch to the living room.

"It's about fucking time," Jack glared at me.

I set his plate on the table. "Would you like another?" I nod toward the empty bottle.

"You're damn right. I want another. You should have brought it with you."

I served him his drink, walked back to the kitchen, and cleaned up. I washed down the counter and the kitchen island and then took out the trash. Satisfied that he would have no complaints, I went out to the patio to rest and calm my nerves.

That's when Molly found me.

***

We are finished with our tea, and it's too hot to stay outside. Molly should leave now that she has imparted the news and gotten as much information from me as she can. But today, she lingers, studying me as I stare at my patio door and wait for the reverend to come.

I smile at Molly, trying to think of anything that would break the silence, and I hear the doorbell ring. Thank goodness, the minister has arrived.

I stand up and walk to the front of the house. Uninvited, Molly follows me. She does have a nose for news.

"Hi," I welcome the reverend. "Come on in; Jack's in the study."

"Jack," I call, "you have company."

He doesn't respond. I didn't expect him to. The noise we hear is the wrestlers on TV slamming each other to the mat.

"Go on in," I urge the Reverend. "I'll get your tea."

Molly follows the reverend. First Molly, then the reverend, gasps. I stop midway to the kitchen. "Is there a problem?" I call.

Molly has backed out of the study and is standing in the hall, staring at me. Her hands cover her mouth. Her eyes are wider than

I've ever seen. She can't speak. A tragic condition for a gossip.

The reverend follows Molly into the hall. "Carrie, I'm so sorry." He is using his low, calm, funeral voice.

"What?" I ask. I barge past them into the study. Jack is lying on the floor where he has fallen. His plate is next to him. Once again, my carpet is littered—this time with chips, bread, ham, cheese, mayo, and a dead husband. One tiny piece of gherkin is lodged in the hand clutching his heart.

"Oh my God." I sink to the floor beside Jack. His skin is still pink, not the dull gray it will turn to in a few hours. He can't have been dead for very long. There is a grimace of pain on his face. I take the gherkin from him and slip it into my pocket. Details, I remind myself.

Molly comes over to comfort me and study the scene for the description she will broadcast throughout the community.

The reverend has called 911 and now he is dialing our local funeral home. "Charlie will come for his body," he tells me. "Would you like me to sit with you?"

Molly nods, forgetting the question isn't aimed at her.

I settled down on a chair facing Jack.

The reverend clears his throat, "Do you want a moment alone with him?"

I shake my head. I have nothing more to say to my husband.

"Perhaps you'd be more comfortable in the living room," the Reverend offers.

Of course, with a dead body in the study, it is not the most comforting place to sit.

Molly is the most reluctant to leave the scene of Jack's untimely death.

I walk out and don't look back. Once we are settled in the living room, I say, "He was a kind man." I choke on the sentiment. What widow wouldn't?

"Yes," Molly joins me in the lie, but her sharp eyes study me. "At least he enjoyed his favorite meal before...well. You know."

"Yes," I agree.

"It was probably a heart attack. I think Jack went quickly with little pain." Reverend Johnson continues to comfort me. "And there won't be any inquiry, considering his age and how out of shape he was. He is lucky to have lived this long."

"And he did get his favorite pickles for his last meal," Molly adds.

"Yes," I nod at her as I try for a weak little smile.

***

It seemed like an eternity before Jack was taken away, and both Reverend Johnson and Molly departed, finally leaving me in peace.

I take the gherkin out of my pocket and drop it into the garbage disposal along with the rest of the jar of Nancy's Fancy Sweet Gherkins. I smile to myself. Jack had helped himself to more of the pickles after I served him lunch. I knew he would.

I rinse the jar with hot water and bleach before dumping it into the garbage. And it's a damn good thing I got the right jar of pickles; I was running out of cyanide. The Devil is in the details.

~*~

HIGH TIMES IN JAVALINA JUNCTION

CYNTHIA SABELHAUS

I limped off the plane, barely noticing the caress of warm, dry air coming through gaps around the jet bridge. My left calf muscle cramped beneath its prosthesis, and I lurched against the wall. This is what I get for running too far, too fast this morning. I'd been trying to teach myself to run again. I didn't care about winning races, but I needed to know I could run faster than a bad guy chasing me. I know. Crazy. Blame it on a decade of service in military and civilian police forces. My fellow passengers rushed past, some muttering, "Excuse me, ma'am."

Body appendages tend to swell with changes in air pressure. My prosthesis was too tight. Biting back a dozen expletives, I hobbled into the terminal. Some of those swallowed epithets were aimed at Jack. He'd called early that morning. From jail. He was accused of murdering someone he said he'd never met. So here I was at Tucson International Airport, enroute to bail out my baby brother.

Given our ten-year age gap, we were never close as kids. Jack was still in elementary school when I left home to join the Army. When I left the Army Criminal Investigation Division to join the

Boston Police, Jack had already headed for Navy Seal training. Unfortunately, a shipboard fire laid him up for a while and ended his Navy career. He moved to Javelina Junction, Arizona—an old mining town and suburb of Tucson—to start a hunting and off-road tourist adventure business.

***

The drive from the airport was only twenty miles, but the road was not a freeway, and the journey lasted over an hour. I navigated endless hairpin curves and inclines, moving through a mountain pass populated by tall, gangly saguaros and patches of purple and gold wildflowers. As the sun touched the horizon, sharp lines of the desert landscape were glorious in the neon sunset.

It was dark when I parked my rental car at the office of a motel masquerading as a collection of log cabins. I knew Javelina Junction's police station and jail were part of the town office complex, which had presumably closed for the day. Jack suggested this motel, Camp Javelina, and was urging me to talk to the owner when his call dropped.

I entered the motel's largest cabin. A wood plaque shaped like a javelina hung next to the door. According to Jack, pig-looking javelinas roamed freely in the Tucson boonies. The cabin held a smoke-stained fireplace and bookcases overflowing with paperbacks and puzzles, as well as a reception desk at one end. A half-dozen tables were scattered among oversized, overstuffed furniture in various shades of fake leather. A sign at the desk announced breakfast service daily from 6-9.

The chubby middle-aged brunette behind the desk wore a big smile and a turquoise caftan befitting the climate. "You must be Meryl," she said, standing and extending her hand.

I hadn't made a reservation and was puzzled about how she knew my name. I closed the distance between us and reached to shake her hand. "What gave me away?"

"I saw your picture at Jack's place. He talks about you all the time." Her eyes strayed to my legs. "He told me about the shoot-out that took your leg. Sometimes I just got to ask what the Good Lord was thinking. He gets you through hell in Afghanistan and then lets a policeman take you down right here in the U.S. of A." She shook her head. "It just don't seem right."

I shrugged and brushed my short blond hair away from my face. "I'm Meryl Collins. I'm afraid Jack didn't tell me your name."

"Stephanie Kominski—call me Steph. I own this place. I met Jack at a chamber of commerce meeting when he started renovating the old gas station down the road. He opened last fall, and from what I hear, he's done well, and my business has increased as a result."

"So, what's the story on Jack being in jail?"

Before Steph could reply, an SUV pulled up, and a family piled out—mother, father, and stair-step kids. Steph frowned, and her voice dropped. "Not now. I got folks coming in most of the night. Besides, there's nothing you can do tonight. Dinner's in your fridge, and I left a bottle of wine on your counter. Meet me here for breakfast anytime after six."

I started to protest over the noise from the check-ins. Steph pushed a key into my hand, forced a smile, and pointed right. "Last cabin. Welcome to Javelina Junction."

A path lit by fairy lights led to the cabins. Mine had a covered porch across the front with three wooden steps, each holding a hand-painted pot of geraniums. The cabin door opened into a living area with a fireplace and kitchenette, and an open door that led to a bedroom and bath. Another porch across the back of the cabin had an expansive view of the valley below, where Tucson lights sprawled from one mountain range to the next. Vacation dreams popped into my head. Not happening.

Despite the rustic appearance, my cabin had Wi-Fi and cable T.V. After unpacking, I nuked the fried chicken dinner Steph mentioned and watched the local news. No murders were reported. A quick Google search yielded nothing about any local murders, either. It was late, and my body was still on Boston time, so I took a quick shower and crashed.

Morning came too soon. I dressed and headed to the office where Steph stood at the reception desk talking to a young man.

It was two minutes to six, and none of the other guests were there yet.

"Good morning," the man called to me. "Food will be out in just a couple of minutes."

Steph patted him on the shoulder. "Meryl is a friend of mine. We're going to have breakfast upstairs. Call me if you need anything."

I followed Steph through a large commercial kitchen and up a set of stairs marked "Staff Only." Upstairs, an elegant foyer ended at an ornate door. Steph took a key from her pocket and opened the door, then stepped aside for me to enter. I walked into an expansive living space that could have been featured in Architectural Digest. An enormous leather sectional took up much of the room while a flatscreen T.V. hung above the fireplace.

"You live up here?" I asked.

"Yes. It's convenient. My work commute is 15 stair steps."

We sat across from each other at a round oak table with overflowing platters of breakfast entrees arranged between us. Steph poured coffee and nodded at the food. "Dig in."

As we worked our way through breakfast, I said, "So, tell me about Jack's problem."

Steph took a sip of coffee. "It's strange. The fellow he's accused of murdering is a doofus named Mateo Romero. He's a distant relative of Gabe Torres, the police chief, but I think Gabe would just as soon see Mateo gone…or dead, not necessarily in that order." She winked at me and continued chewing. "They're not close."

"How did Mateo die?"

Steph mumbled through a large bite of gravy-ed biscuit. "Nobody knows."

"Huh?"

"No body."

"So, how do they know he's dead?"

Steph pointed her fork at me. "That's the question. Rumor has it they found blood at Jack's place. All I know is Chief Torres arrested Jack late the night before last. Jack might know more by now." She paused while I looked down the barrel of her fork.

"Watch your backside, Meryl. The chief has two deputies. All three of 'em are meaner than rattlesnakes. If there's any crime happening in Javelina Junction, my money's on the cops being behind it."

I nodded, stood, and thanked Steph for the food and the info.

***

I was at the door to the police station at nine a.m. when it opened. The policeman at the desk was fortyish, short and wiry. The name patch over his uniform shirt pocket said Hanson. His eyes measured my chest, never made it to my face.

"I'd like to visit my brother, Jack Collins."

That brought his eyes up a few inches, still not meeting mine. "No can do, little lady."

"And why is that? Do you have regular visiting hours?"

"Nope. No visitors. Chief's orders. You might as well get your sweet ass back in that Chevy Blazer and head on home."

So, he'd scoped out my car. "Can you give me the name of Jack's attorney?"

"Doesn't have one, so far as I know."

I turned to leave, hating to expose my sweet ass to his beady little eyes. At the door, I turned and grimaced. "I'll be back."

***

I drove a couple miles, then pulled off the two-lane road and dialed Steph. She answered on the first ring.

"Hi, Steph. It's Meryl. Can you recommend a good lawyer?"

"Not in Javelina Junction, but I've been told there's a good one on this side of Tucson. I don't know him personally, but I've heard good things. His name is Jeremiah Anders." There was a pause. "I just texted you his number."

"Thanks."

"How's Jack doing?" she asked.

"I don't know. Deputy Hanson wouldn't let me see him—said the chief was not allowing visitors."

"Swine! The whole herd of 'em. You be careful, Meryl."

"Always."

I was surprised when the lawyer answered my call. He told me to call him Jerry and gave me directions. Twenty minutes later, I arrived at a small storefront in a strip mall. There was a receptionist's desk near the entrance, but no receptionist. The door behind the desk was partially open, and I heard a phone ring and a man answer.

The phone was on "speaker" and Steph's voice was loud. "She been there yet?"

"No. But don't worry, I'll handle it. Mateo turn up?"

"Not that I've heard. Some critter probably dragged him off."

"Okay. Stay cool."

So, Steph does know this lawyer. Why did she say otherwise? I stepped back outside, counted to ten, then went in, making more noise than necessary as I slammed the door behind me.

Jerry stepped out of his office door and invited me in. As soon as I told him what I knew of Jack's situation, he started packing his briefcase.

"I'm a trained investigator, Jerry. How can I help?"

Jerry looked at me for a moment. "You might want to swing by Jack's business and see if there's any evidence of a search, any blood, you know, the usual. I'd also like to know whether Mateo Romero is even missing. He lives out on Coyote Trail with his wife and a couple kids. Could you go out there and see what his wife has to say? Annie's a sweet girl and will probably insist on feeding you cookies."

I replayed Jerry's and Steph's conversation but wasn't sure what it all meant. I figured there was no harm in visiting Mateo's place, so I fed Coyote Trail into my phone's GPS app and headed there first. If Mateo wasn't missing, Jack should be able to walk out of that jail today. I'd check Jack's place later.

***

The street was a winding unpaved two-track between scrubby desert trees. Mateo's place didn't have a street number on it, but it was the only house I'd seen. It was small and neat, with a raked dirt yard and children's bicycles lined up near the porch. I hadn't quite made it to the door when it opened, and a young woman stepped out.

"Mrs. Romero?"

She nodded.

"I'm Meryl Collins. I was wondering whether you'd talk to me about your husband. I understand he's missing."

As Jerry predicted, she opened the door wider and invited me in, led me to the kitchen, and stopped to clear the square Formica table of cereal bowls and breadcrumbs. "The kids were late for the bus this morning. Normally they clean off the table. Sit down. I'll pour us some coffee. Cream or sugar?"

"Black for me, but please don't go to any trouble."

She smiled shyly behind long straight blond hair and put steaming mugs on the table before sitting across from me. "Mattie went to work three days ago, and he hasn't been back. He does that. We don't have a phone here at the house, and sometimes his boss sends him to pick up materials from Casa Grande or Nogales." She smiled. "I'm not worried about him. We're soulmates. I'd know if anything were wrong."

"What does Mateo do?"

"Mostly concrete work for roads and buildings. Sometimes he drives a truck—picks up and delivers stuff."

Annie insisted on packing me three cookies for the road. She handed me a note along with the goodies. "If you see Mattie, would you give him this?"

I nodded, hoping her husband was alive—for both our sakes.

***

When I braked at the highway, I noticed a text from Jerry. He'd cleared the way for me to see Jack and asked me to call him afterward. So, next stop, the police station, then Jack's place.

This time my reception at the police station had a veneer of politeness. The chief was in residence. He was in his late forties, not tall, but fit, with the kind of warm brown eyes that drew you in. Gabe Torres walked from his office and shook my hand. Deputy Hanson still sat at the front counter, still stared at my chest.

"Nice to meet you, Ms. Collins. They're bringing your brother up from the cells. I'll walk you back to the interview room."

"Thanks." I broke eye contact as soon as I could.

The chief unlocked a door and held it open for me. Jack was already seated at the metal table. Once the door was closed, he glanced up at the camera. I saw a flash of red. "Sis. It's good to see you."

I took a seat across from him. "You too, kiddo."

"You staying at Camp Javelina?"

"Yep. It's nice. The owner seems friendly." I hadn't figured out how we were going to communicate.

"You mind checking on my place? I'm not sure they locked the doors after they scooped me up. Have the cops give you my valuables. The keys should be in there."

Is Jack telling me to find something at his place? "You need anything?"

"No. I'm good. You remember when I caught that little trout when I was about four or five, and I tried to keep it alive?"

And now I know where to look. "How could I forget?" I forced a laugh. "You were one goofy brat." I stood. "I'll be back later, little brother. What can I bring you?"

"A book to read. It's pretty boring down there in the basement."

"You got it."

I pounded on the door and waited for someone to let me out. I asked Hanson for my brother's valuables. He complied, and I was on the road again.

Back in my cabin, I called Steph. She told me Jack's place was a half-mile down the road. I decided to walk. After pulling on hiking boots and a baseball cap, I searched the kitchen drawers for a weapon. A clunky pocketknife would have to do. I stuck it in one jeans pocket along with Jack's keys. My silenced phone went into the other.

I was sweating when I reached Jack's business. It looked more Swiss chalet than old gas station. I skirted the building and used his key to open the back door. Locking it behind me, I checked the front door. Not locked. I fixed that.

Jack's story about the small fish never happened. He had a stuffed Northern pike, and I'd always teased him about its size. It wasn't prize-worthy. I found his office and saw the pike hanging above his desk. I could see a bit of paper in the fish's mouth. I pulled it out and recognized the numbers written on it. Jack's memory was mush, but seriously? 7-1-7-8-7. He couldn't remember my birthday? But it might also be the combination to a safe.

What had he said after the bit about the fish? He wanted a book. The safe could be inside a book or behind several volumes. I explored his office but found few books. There was a pine staircase next to the back wall. I went up. The door on the landing at the top of the stairs was locked. On the third try, I found the right key and went in, locking the door behind me. It might buy me time if someone broke in downstairs.

Unlike Steph's place, Jack's tiny living room held one worn recliner and about ten bookcases. Great. I moved along each row of books, pulling out a handful here and there to look behind them. In the last bookcase, I hit paydirt—a wall safe. Using the combination from the pike, I twirled it open. In addition to Jack's personal papers, there was a thick folder. I took it to the desk and began flipping the pages. It looked like Jack had stumbled upon a marijuana crop. He had it circled on a map, and he'd taken photos of Chief Torres and Deputy Hanson standing near a forest of tall, healthy marijuana plants sheltered by an umbrella of scrawny desert trees. I photographed each page with my phone and sent them to Jerry, assuming he might use them to spring Jack.

I put the folder away, locked the safe, and replaced the books in front of it.

The doorbell chimed downstairs. I peeked out the window

and saw an older white Chevy pickup in the driveway. The person ringing the bell was hidden beneath the overhanging porch roof. I froze. Maybe they'll go away.

"Meryl? You here?"

I recognized Steph's voice and started down the stairs. Had she seen me leave the cabin? The bell rang again. I unlocked and opened the door. "Steph? What's up?"

She looked into the room behind me. "I got worried. You've been gone a long time."

I walked out the door before she could step inside. "I'm done here. Mind giving me a ride back to the camp?"

"Nope." We walked onto the porch, and I locked the front door. When we got into her truck, she asked, "You find anything interesting?"

"It was fun to poke around Jack's new business, but no. I didn't find a thing that could help him with his current problem."

Steph's eyebrows went up, but she smiled. "Well, I'm glad you're okay. You can't imagine what I was thinking." She took one hand off the wheel to pat my arm.

Something felt off. My instincts hummed as we parked near the office. I got out and turned toward my cabin. "Thanks for caring and for the ride," I said over my shoulder. "I want to take a shower. It's a lot hotter here than I'm used to."

Steph looked like she wanted me to stay, but she waved and turned toward the office.

Once inside my cabin, I filled a tall glass with ice water and let my brain drift. What did I really know? Jack found an illegal marijuana operation. He took pictures of the police chief and deputy inspecting the plants. The question was: were they growing the plants, or had they discovered the farm as Jack had? Nothing in those photos proved it either way.

And I'd sent the photos to Jerry. A mistake? Instincts hummed louder.

I walked to the front window. Why was I suddenly suspicious of everyone I met here? I glanced toward the motel office just as a VW Passat pulled into the parking lot and swung around the building. Jerry was driving, but he wasn't headed toward my room. The office had a back door. Jerry and Steph? Steph had recommended him to me. She'd claimed not to know him, but that proved untrue.

I got up and paced the room. Okay. If Steph and Jerry are up to something, what does that say about the local cops? I dialed the police station.

Chief Torres answered, and I asked to speak to Jack.

"He's right here," the chief said. "I've got you on speaker."

What is Jack doing "right here?" And where is "here?" The chief's office or an interview room?

Jack interrupted my thoughts. "Meryl? You okay?"

"Fine, I think." I tried to figure out the puzzle. Finally, I asked, "So, are the cops the good guys or the bad guys?"

Jack laughed. "Definitely the good guys."

"And Steph and Jerry?"

The chief spoke up. "Why do you ask?"

I looked out the window. "I found your file, Jack, and I sent the pics to your lawyer. He went straight to Steph, and now they're both headed my way. I think I might need backup here."

The chief replied. "We're on our way, Ms. Collins. Are you at the motel?"

"The cabin closest to town," I said just as Steph knocked. "I'm going to leave my phone on. You might be able to hear what's happening." I didn't wait for a reply, left the phone transmitting, and slid it under yesterday's newspaper in the waste basket.

Steph hollered from the front porch, "Steph and Jerry here. You decent?"

I walked over and opened the door. "Come in. Can I get anybody some water? Coffee?"

"Sorry, Meryl," Steph said. "I got a call from a friend in town. The chief and his crew are headed for the field Jack found. Jerry showed me the pictures. I think we can beat them there and maybe stop them or get photos of them hiding the evidence. Are you game?"

I was willing to bet nobody had called Steph. So, why do they want me out in that field? And could the chief hear what she said? I moved closer to my hidden phone and bent to retie a shoe.

"Shouldn't we call someone? Let them know we're heading out to wherever this field is?"

Jerry spoke up. "Already done, but we can't be sure the state police will be there before the Javelina Junction cops show up."

Steph opened the cabin door. "Come on, you two. We'll take my truck. It's parked outside the office."

I reached for my purse, but Jerry took my elbow and hustled me to the door.

I was jammed between Jerry and Steph on the bench seat of the old Chevy half-ton. Its shocks were shot, something I hadn't noticed on our half-mile trip from Jack's. The drive to the field took fifteen minutes. My tailbone was bruised by the time we parked in the cactus and dried grass overlooked by rock outcroppings. I guessed the field must be on the other side of the rocks.

I looked around. "I hope the state police can find this place."

Steph opened her door and got out. "Let's go," she said to Jerry.

Jerry got out, half-dragging me behind him.

"Hey, take it easy." I pulled away from him as soon as my feet hit the ground. "Shouldn't we wait for backup?"

Steph had already moved around the rocks. Jerry took my arm. Clearly, we weren't waiting. I slowed my pace, faked a stumble, slowed more, limped. Jerry didn't loosen his grip, but he was looking everywhere but at me. What a weasel. I stood taller and looked up at Steph. "So, this is your farm? Yours and Jerry's?"

"A little slow, but she finally gets there," Steph called back to Jerry.

I looked at Jerry. "And you didn't call the cops."

He didn't answer, just looked at Steph, waiting for her to take the lead.

I wondered whether the chief and his guys were close. Surely, they couldn't have been more than a few minutes behind us. I wasn't sure about local geography, but the field seemed to be equidistant from town and Steph's place. I looked up at Steph. "Why would you risk everything to grow marijuana?"

Steph frowned. "Why would I not? Without the extra income,

70

I would have lost the motel two years ago. Nobody was taking vacations, and the bank was threatening foreclosure. The fields paid my mortgage when the visitors didn't. Nobody got hurt, and I survived."

"What about Mateo? Did he get hurt?" This time I didn't look at Jerry. I need to do this one at a time. I took a deep breath, squared my shoulders, and kneed Jerry's groin to make him let my arm go. He recovered fast, but I was moving faster. I ran straight for Steph.

"That's enough!" Steph grabbed my right wrist and pulled me toward her.

Not a smart move, Steph. This is one of the first defense tactics taught in every police academy and MP school. My response was automatic. I placed my left hand over her fingers, held on tight, and swung both my arms in an arc, ending with Steph's arm behind her back. By pushing down on her hyper-extended elbow, I slammed her face-down to the ground.

But Jerry was still loose. Where's that backup? While I had Steph down, with my right knee on her back and her arm bent into a handcuff position, I couldn't do much about Jerry. I watched him pick up a fallen tree branch about the size of a baseball bat. He rushed me, both hands throttling the branch, looking like he intended to reach for the bleachers using my head as the ball. I leaned right, kicked out with my left leg, and managed to snag him behind the knees. He came down hard and I stomped on his ankle for good measure. I had no sense for how much force I'd used, but I was glad my artificial foot had no pain receptors. My stump would be bruised.

Jerry crawled toward me, but when I pulled out the pocketknife and opened the miniature blade, he cowered and fussed with his ankle. Steph bucked but couldn't dislodge me. And the cavalry finally came over the hill.

Later, at the Javelina Junction Police Station, I signed my statement and collected Jack. The chief escorted us to his office and gestured toward chairs alongside a young man he introduced as Mateo.

Mateo mumbled that he had stumbled into the marijuana

operation while trying to pilfer a baby saguaro to surprise his wife. Speaking painfully, through bruised and swollen lips, he described being beaten unconscious, bound and gagged, and half-buried in a shallow grave. By early the next day, he'd freed his hands, pushed back the dirt, and walked three miles to the highway. He flagged down a passing motorist who took him to the police station. The chief heard Mateo's story and put him in protective custody. Mateo hadn't seen his attackers' faces, so the police still had no idea who was behind the operation.

The next day, Chief Torres and Deputy Hanson drove out to the area Mateo had described and found the pot farm. Jack happened on the fields while he was scouting javelina hunting sites for the fall season. He spotted the chief at the same time he realized what was growing there. He took pictures and tried to slip away.

But Chief Torres saw Jack driving away and thought it best to hold both Mateo and Jack in protective custody pending investigation to determine who was behind the marijuana farm and the attack on Mateo. Jack's innocence was in question until Steph stepped up to take the credit. Jerry was laundering Steph's pot profits and taking a cut for himself.

If Jerry hadn't come at me with that bat-branch, his denials might have been believed. Instead, Jerry and Steph were both in federal lockup in Tucson pending arraignment and likely huge bail bonds—Lady Justice frowns on lawyers gone wrong and their accomplices.

"But why did Jerry threaten me?" I asked.

Chief Torres smiled. "Jerry thought you overheard a call from Steph at his office."

I wasn't so clever after all. Damned instincts. I shrugged.

The chief warned Mateo about stealing cactus, then cut us loose. On the way out of the station, Deputy Hanson apologized. "The chief told me to act like a jerk—incompetent and creepy so you'd underestimate us. Sorry about that."

I smiled. "You gave an Oscar-worthy performance, Deputy."

We caught up with Mateo on the sidewalk. "Hey, Mateo," I called out. "I almost forgot. I've got a note from your wife."

He read it aloud. "Milk, eggs, butter. I guess I should get her a cell phone."

I waved as he made his way to the market.

With Steph behind bars and the motel padlocked, I crashed on a cot at Jack's that night and drove to Tucson the next morning. I was anxious to get back home to my little Boston restaurant, Soup, but glad to know my baby brother was doing well in his new career. He thought he might put in a bid for Steph's motel, and I promised to come back soon for a real vacation.

IT'S GOOD TO BE ALIVE?
Based on a True Story

ELAINE A. POWERS

Pusch Ridge faded from purple to black as night engulfed the Santa Catalina Mountains. He waited. He would only emerge from his den when the last rays of sunlight were gone. "Hunting's best in the dark," he whispered from the shadows. He cleaned and sharpened his weapons, brushing them until they gleamed, if there had been moonlight for them to gleam in. The repetitive movements both relaxed and enhanced his desires.

Surveying his surroundings, he analyzed his hunger. "What will satisfy my needs tonight?" He roamed cautiously, eager, but aware of the dangers that the night concealed. Fear. Fear of what couldn't be seen heightened all his senses. His prey must not hear his approach. A cricket chirped loudly nearby. Good, a welcome distraction. His padded soles reduced his light step even more. He always stepped cautiously on the hard desert soil.

Tonight, he did not wander. He knew where his intended victim resided. Despite the new moon's darkness, he moved confidently, sensing his way. He was experienced at stalking. He would wait for the right moment to move in for the kill, despite his all-consuming need to consume. He paused mid-step. Yes, he had felt a vibration through the ground. His prey was out and moving.

"There," he said softly to himself and resumed his approach. He was unconcerned that his soon-to-be victim would hear him coming. Unlike his noisy prey, he knew he wouldn't be heard; he truly was death approaching on "cat's paws."

He paused, lurking behind his prey, waiting, savoring the moment. The breeze ruffled his hair. Tense, he carefully placed one foot closer...then leapt forward, immediately driving his blades deep into the startled body. He pinned his victim to the ground with his body, preventing escape. His powerful hold energized him. He was revitalized as the victim's life flowed out.

He took what he wanted from the body, discarding the remains to desiccate in the dry desert air. "Perhaps a scavenger will appreciate my success." The male walked boldly toward his home; no stealth needed now. "Yes, an excellent night's hunt. I am a predator. I should be feared. Everyone, beware!"

Satiated, he thought of another prey he might seek: a mate. Yes, another pursuit would begin soon. "It's good to be alive."

***

She was pleased with the change in the male's demeanor. Of course, it didn't matter to her if he stayed in the shadows or not. "You can't hide you from me." Had she been a compassionate creature, she would have appreciated his enjoyment of his last meal...but she was not compassionate.

She didn't need to hide; camouflaged as she was in black with rust-colored accents, she blended with her surroundings. Moving confidently, she approached the unwary male. She circled the area, deciding on the best location. She would take the killer by surprise, subdue him quickly by necessity. Even though she was tall and slim, the female was still quite small in comparison to her intended victim. Like the male, she had prepared for her night's hunt. He used killer strength, but she had enhanced weapons.

"Take your time, prey, I'm patient," she whispered. She ascended to the top of a rock overlooking his approach. She perched, poised, ready for her assault.

Her prey seemed to be walking directly into her trap. She tensed. Almost…almost…but then he wandered away to examine something off to his left. She shivered in frustration. "No problem, everything comes to she who waits." She couldn't see what had attracted his attention, but she was rewarded by his return to his original route. "Yes, come to me. I'm waiting for you. I will wait all night for you."

When he reached her ambush spot, she launched off the rock onto the male, grinding him into the dirt. Her long legs encircled his body, as she plunged her weapon easily through his skin. Her poison was forced into the wound. He bucked and writhed, but the toxin quickly took effect. The family recipe, with a few special ingredients of her own, never failed. The killer calmed and no longer fought. She released her grip and moved aside to admire her handiwork. Her intent was not to kill the male immediately. She merely needed to render him compliant. She had plans for his magnificent body.

The female looked around to see if anyone who might interfere was near. After all, only half her job was done. She hovered over her quiet victim. Her special mixture paralyzed his limbs, but not the rest of his bodily functions. His lungs and his brain continued their work. "You should be honored. Your life will now serve the most important purpose."

She confirmed that he couldn't resist and grabbed hold of his head. Despite their size difference, her strong leg muscles easily moved the male's larger body.

"I apologize for the rough drag, my dear. I will try not to hit too many rocks. My place isn't very far away. Then you can rest." His leg snagged on the lower branch of a bush, but she jerked him loose.

"Here we are," she said as she pulled her victim inside her work area. She arranged his body, admiring his physique. She extended his limbs away from his torso, which she examined thoroughly. She checked for injuries that the transit might have caused. "Good, you are undamaged. You are suitable."

She looked in the male's eyes. "Don't worry, I'm not going to eat you." She chuckled. "I'll be leaving, but you won't be alone." Selecting a specific area, she cut a small hole in the male's abdomen. With his limbs paralyzed, he could not thrash, despite the pain. She paused, admiring the opening. "Perfect. Not too big, not too small."

Pushing the cut edges apart, she inserted her gift. She manipulated his abdomen to close the wound. "There, all done. You won't die for a long time yet. And very soon, you won't be alone."

With one last tap on his abdomen, she left, sealing her work area entrance behind her. She had other victims to find, one for each her precious gifts.

***

Was it still good to be alive?

The male languished, alive and alone...until the female's gift hatched. The egg's occupant emerged within the male's body and fed enthusiastically. The male's vital organs were eaten last, to ensure the freshness of its food. When nothing was left of the killer-turned-host, the male was released into death. The larva pupated, transforming, and maturing. The now-adult tarantula hawk wasp emerged from the male tarantula's corpse to perpetuate the cycle of life and death.

It was good to be alive!

~*~

TRIPLE DANG

CONDA DOUGLAS

Dang. Getting older and a mite forgetful sure isn't easy. Neither is being dependent on technology.

I sighed as I parked in the Straight Shooting Range parking lot. If my phone isn't here, I don't know where it'd be. And I'm already late opening the Open Carry Bar. Luckily, I own the bar, so's it's not that big of a problem. This early in the day, my only customer will be Beer-loving Bob anyway.

Jeff looked up at the front desk when I entered. "Here ya go, Julie." He reached underneath the counter, then placed my phone on top. Whew.

"Thanks. See you on Monday." I nodded and snatched my forgotten absolutely necessary technology, turned to head out and paused. The rich, delightful aromas of gunpowder and gun oil wafted on the air and made my nose tingle, while the muted sound of intermittent gunfire tickled my ears.

This early on a weekday morning gunfire could mean only one thing. My boyfriend Tim must be giving a private lesson. Always missing my man, me, when we're both working our long hours.

I should go, but what the heck, I was already late. Bob could wait. Bob would wait. I turned back and said, "I'll just take a peek at Tim and his student."

Jeff straightened. "Um, well, but—"

I gave him a reassuring wave as I headed back. "No worries, I won't interrupt. Just look through the door window."

"But—" Jeff's voice floated after me as I walked down the long hallway to one of the inside target ranges.

Standing on my toes, I peered through the wired, reinforced door glass. And swallowed a gasp.

I expected to see Tim standing next to his student and, well, teaching them how to shoot. Or maybe assisting by standing behind and reaching around his student and showing how to hold the gun in the proper position. His job. Instead, he wrapped his corded-muscle arms around a pretty, plump, golden-haired, big-boobed woman, about my age, kissing her full on the mouth.

Dang.

I turned away before they saw me watching and staggered out to the front counter. Jeff stared at me, his eyebrows pulled down tight, making me think of a laser of concern beaming my way. I couldn't have him know what I'd just seen. Not until I'd digested the horrid sight. Maybe vomited it up a few times.

"My lord," I said, managing what I hoped was a convincing grin and not a grimace, "Tim's such a great teacher, looks like I'll have some tough competition in the next Shoot Straight Awards."

Jeff gave a real smile, looking relieved that Tim and that woman weren't smooching as he feared, and I'd seen them. "Yup, Susha sure can shoot."

Susha? What kind of name is that? A man-stealing name for sure.

"And it's only her second lesson," Jeff added.

Her second lesson? Double dang. She learned fast and moved fast on men.

All I could do was nod and give what I hoped was a cheery wave as I left.

Triple dang.

***

80

Cuss words. Lots of 'em.

I polished that one spot on the bar top so long and hard it shone lighter in the varnish. I stared down at my gleaming antique oak. What to do? What to—

"Beer me, Julie," Bob, our resident alcoholic, or rather beer-a-holic, called from his permanent spot at the opposite end of the bar.

I welcomed the interruption to my spinning, spiraling thoughts. And the command to do something, anything.

"Last one," I said, drawing him another IPA draft, his favorite, smiling, watching the perfect head on the beer form. Forty-plus years of practice paid off.

Bob's wet lower lip protruded, a petulant, if tipsy, toddler. "Why? It's only my third and I'm walking home."

"It's your sixth."

"But I'm your only customer," Bob said.

"For now." I looked out at the empty old oak tables, placed just the way I like them, all set up and waiting. Pristine. Perfect. Just the way it should be. Lordy, I love owning my own bar. My own successful bar.

Open Carry started out over a century ago as a bucket-of-blood bar outside Tucson. By the time I started as a teenage dishwasher in the kitchen in the late 70s, Tucson had grown around it and the bar had gone all disco, ugh. In my decades of working here, the bar went through several permutations—once even serving bad Chinese food with the beer and whiskey—and several attendant bankruptcies.

Not going to happen with Open Carry. Faced with yet another spate of unemployment and inspired by the brand-new shooting range a few blocks away, I spent all my savings to buy the bar. I rested my hand on my sidearm. My idea worked. Can I niche-market or what?

Bob interrupted my pride fest with, "Fourth beer." He spoke as if we were in a bidding war.

"Sixth and last." I narrowed my eyes in my best woman-with-a-gun-on-her-hip glare.

"Fifth." Bob never gave up when it came to alcohol.

"Drink up before I take it away." Now I wondered if maybe a few more moments of alone time might help me figure out what to do about Tim and my competition. I'm of an age, downhill tumble from 60, where good, healthy, single men are rare as roofers in monsoon season. Tim was a two-timing son of a gun instead of a straight shooter, but I could skip that one part. Get a bit long in the tooth and it's easier to overlook things. Sometimes.

Bob looked stricken at my threat. He wrapped his hands around the beer glass.

I softened my tone with, "In a few minutes I've got to get ready for the lunch hour. Fridays, ya know."

"It's not Friday, it's Monday, nobody comes in on Monday morning, save me," Bob said, breaking into my musings again.

That was why Monday was Tim's and my day to date. After I took a now-unnecessary, but kissingly fun, private lesson from him, we'd head somewhere not-my-bar for lunch and drinks, and great afternoon sex afterward. I always paid for the boozy lunch—a tip to Tim for great private lessons. Private lessons, just like the lesson I'd witnessed this morning. How he kept us separate, I supposed. He knew all the ins and outs of my work schedule.

Mondays, my newest bartender Erica, worked the long hours from noon opening until midnight closing. She didn't mind. She got plenty of time from noon to six to study for her college classes, and time-and-a-half for four hours overtime to pay for those classes.

"No, Bob." I reiterated, "It's Friday."

Bob sat back on his stool, swayed for a moment, then righted himself. Long-term drinker ability. "Friday? Really?" He put his hand on his empty holster. Everyone else in Open Carry could, well, open carry. Not Bob, never Bob. Too tipsy, too risky. As a sop to his feelings, I allowed him an empty holster—so he could say that he forgot his pistol at home. Totally believable with Bob.

I leaned forward. Big mistake. A waft of stale craft beer and unwashed teeth blasted my face. Bob always paid his bill, so he had enough money to spring for a toothbrush and toothpaste. Why he didn't avail himself of those two tools, I didn't know. I leaned back and said, "Yup, it's Friday."

"Hunh. It is my sixth beer." Bob got out his wallet, paid the right amount with a generous tip, as always, slid off the stool and said, "See you tomorrow."

I nodded, already lost in what-to-do-about-Tim-and-that-slut land. I didn't get very far in my musings as Roger, my capable cook, held the door for Bob to go out—and Susha, my competition, to come in.

Oh sh—shoot.

Shooting Susha seemed like a possible solution, and my hand was partway to my holster before I realized that I'd have to shoot Roger, too. Couldn't leave witnesses. Couldn't do without my cook, either. With a head shake—must be shock at thinking these thoughts—I plastered a smile on my face and called out, "Welcome to Open Carry. Take a seat anywhere and I'll be right with you."

"Thanks, Hon," Susha called back in a deep, smooth voice, with a light Texas twang. She sat down in a table close to the old stone fireplace that never got used. Why a fireplace in Tucson? Course, I'd never gotten around to removing it, either.

I grabbed one of our bar food menus and headed her way. Stay cool and calm and don't kill her—yet, I told myself.

She reached for the menu with, "This is a great place, love the artwork." She used the menu to gesture at one of Carla's portraits.

On my walls hung the visages of famous gunmen, gunslingers, and marksmen of the past, painted by my forever-best-friend Carla, in her signature half-traditional, half-Andy-Warhol style. Wild Bill Hickok, Wyatt Earp, Annie Oakley, and others stared out from their shadowboxes. Each box held a sawn-in-half gun, representative of whatever weapon that particular notable used. Carla's unique touch. Lord, I loved that woman and her art.

Part of my niche marketing of Open Carry.

My smile became wide and real. Maybe I won't ever kill Susha, just figure out a way to keep this new, appreciative, customer and my boyfriend. Back to whirling thoughts of how.

"Your first time here?" I suspected the answer would be yes, but better to know for sure. Had Tim been bringing her here?

Wouldn't that be too risky? Except for Mondays, when Tim and I were off getting off, I pretty much lived here. It's my bar.

"Sure is," Susha confirmed. "Checking this place out, cuz it's close to Shooting Straight," here she tapped her holster on her hip. She glanced down at the menu and its list of hamburgers and nachos, good salty food that goes great with a beer or two or three. "And the prices seem more reasonable than the places I take my boyfriend, Tim."

I winced as I recalled that I always paid for Tim's food and drinks, too.

Susha thankfully misinterpreted my cringing. She waved a long-purple-nailed hand. "Oh, I have more resources than he does. I was a successful bar singer down in Houston." She looked around at my place. "In fact, I've another reason to check this place out."

I raised my eyebrows.

"Is there a time I can speak to the owner or manager?"

My eyebrows climbed higher. I drew myself up. "I'm the owner."

Susha grinned. "Great. I thought it might take a smart, older woman to think of and create this place."

I liked her more and more.

"Anyway," Susha continued, "I've been missing my gigs. How's about I sing here a couple of nights a week? For tips?" She crooned the first line of the old Western song, "She Done Took My Man," in a deep, husky, beautiful voice.

Brought tears to my eyes and an urge to smack her. Then apologize. Then hire her. Then fire her. Maybe. Holy Moses, why's she so nice and talented? She might bring in more customers. I could always use more customers.

"I could stand before the fireplace," she said.

Get some use out of it, I thought.

"So, what do you say?" Susha held out her hand.

I stared at the proffered, slightly sunburned hand—difficult for newcomers to realize they needed to stay out of all of the sunshine—my mouth open. What to say? I'd love to have you sing if you leave my boyfriend?

84

Susha started to close her fingers. "It's fine to say no."

I scrambled for words. "That's not what I—" A passel of customers came in, loud and boisterous, saving me from gabbling some sort of answer. I looked around to signal Erica and didn't see her. Where was she? She was never late. To Susha, I held up one finger in a wait-a-moment gesture, smiled, nodded and turned to my new guests.

While I grabbed menus, I realized Susha was sure easy to talk to. Maybe I should just talk to her. Maybe I could convince her to leave Tim and then forgive the bastard, or maybe I'll convince myself that I don't care about him anymore. Um, maybe. Worst case, maybe I'll just shoot her and make it look like she drew her weapon. Naw, just kidding. I think.

More people arrived, two big groups. Friday lunch crunch. I gave Susha a wave as I raced by. I couldn't talk to her with all these people around. And, I worried, what had happened to Erica?

As if she psychically heard me, Erica rushed through the front door, frowning, lips tightly compressed. She raced behind the bar and flapped her hand in my direction, in a come-hither gesture.

"I'm sorry, I'm sorry," she said as I came up to her. She kept her head ducked down. In shame? For the first time ever she was late, and only by a few minutes?

"It's okay," I said.

Erica covered her mouth with one hand. "No, it's not." She tried to tie on her apron with the other hand.

I grasped that hand and leaned toward my newest and youngest staff member. "What's wrong?"

She lowered the hand over her mouth. "I broke a tooth this morning." She pulled back her lips.

Sure enough, her top front tooth showed a small chip in one corner. "It's hardly noticeable."

"It's huge." Erica looked about to burst into a Tucson thunderboomer's worth of tears.

Too late I remembered when I was her age how concerned I was with every aspect of my appearance, no matter how small and insignificant. I tied Erica's apron at the back while I reassured her, "Most people won't notice and it's an easy dental fix."

She whirled around, catching my hand in the tie loop.

"Hey, wait," I said, disentangling myself.

"I called my dentist, but she can't take me until Monday at 11:15 am," Erica babbled over my "Hey, wait."

Monday, close to our noon opening. I looked out at Susha, who gave a small smile and wave. Empty Monday mornings—a perfect time to have a private discussion. If Erica had the morning off—

"Can I have Monday morning off?" Erica asked, echoing my thought.

Before I could say yes, she added, "There's hardly ever anybody here. Maybe we could close the bar for an hour or two?"

That sparked an even better idea in my mind. An idea that would make it possible for Susha and me to have a private conversation.

I looked at Erica's wide-eyed, mouth-covered face and said, "No worries, I'll spell you on Monday morning for however long the dentist takes." I'd call Tim and cancel our standing Monday lunch, saying I had to drive to Phoenix for an appointment and would be gone all day.

"But that's your day off," Erica protested. A good employee.

"I'm the owner, I don't get days off." I held up an admonishing finger. "But you have to promise me you'll not cover your mouth while you're working."

Erica winced.

"Hon, that just draws attention to your teeth. Give a big smile and no one will notice the chip."

She slowly lowered her hand and gave a tight-lipped grimace only slightly resembling a smile.

I sighed and nodded. Best I could hope for, I supposed. "Get to work," I said and headed over to Susha's table. I crouched down so I was eye-to-eye with the woman. "Listen, we're headed into the weekend crush right now. I'm going to be swamped until Monday. Can you come in Monday at 11:45 am so we can discuss the details of your singing here?" Fifteen minutes before opening would be enough time, I hoped.

Please say "Yes" so I can stop Tim's cheating, one way or

another—and maybe gain an attraction for Open Carry.

Susha did one better. She put a thumb up and nodded, then pointed at another table, this one packed with customers ready to order.

Dang, I liked this Tim-smooching woman.

***

Monday morning, 11:40 am. My bar. My empty bar. Good so far.

For the fifth time, I fingered the faux-pearl buttons on my best plaid Western-style shirt and smoothed my over-the-knee jean skirt, then adjusted my extra-fancy-carved holster. I'd left off the Open Carry apron too. Wanted to look my best for my upcoming confrontation.

I'd tried telling myself my dress didn't matter a whit, but that was telling myself a lie. I wanted to look better than Susha, or at least as good. It'd make it easier to convince her to leave Tim. To me.

My rival knocked on the front door's glass. I jumped and glanced at the wall clock, the one with pistols as the hands. Right on time.

Before she arrived, I'd pulled a table separate from the others and placed two chairs there across from each other. Now, I forced what I hoped resembled a welcoming smile on my face, opened my front door and gestured to the table. "Let's sit ourselves down and talk."

"Much thanks," Susha said.

You might not be thanking me in a minute, I thought.

Susha sat. She placed a folder on the table and opened it to reveal photos of herself singing in different outfits, all Western-themed. "Here's some of the outfits I was thinking of wearing, plus my well-holstered pistol, of course."

I sat opposite her and leaned forward. "We'll get to that, but first," might as well plunge in, "leave my boyfriend, Tim, alone."

She leaned away from me and placed her hand on the open

87

folder. "You've been seeing my Tim, too?"

My Tim? My Tim? Oh, I didn't think so. "How long have you even been in Tucson, Tex?"

Susha stood, pushing away her chair. "Tex? Is that a slur?"

"With you it is." I stood, too. "I've been with Tim for a year, ever since I opened this bar and started taking lessons at Straight Shooting."

"Then he's tired of tired-old-you." She showed her teeth, and not in a smile.

"Or wants to mooch off of you and love me." Hang on a hot Tucson moment, did I really want a man who mooched off anyone, no matter who?

Before I could mention this thought Susha said, "I'm not going to give Tim up." She took another step back and rested her hand on her holster. "No reason I should to an ancient, scrawny, skanky bar maid."

Ancient? Scrawny? Skanky? Excuse me? Nope, excuse Susha, and no excuse for her boyfriend-stealing soul.

I pulled off the trigger guard on my holster and grabbed the butt of my pistol. "There's no reason I'll ever surrender to a fat, sunburned-to-a-crisp, purple-clawed cheating cow." I pursed my lips and then went, "Moooo . . ."

Susha drew her gun. I drew mine. She aimed. I aimed. And—

The door opened. In came Tim. With his arm tight around Carla, one hand on her boob.

"Carla?" I asked. My voice quivered, just a bit. I tightened my lips and lowered my weapon.

"Who's Carla?" Susha asked while mimicking my action. Good gun safety.

My friend shook herself free of Tim's embrace. "You told me you weren't dating Julie anymore." She took a few steps away from the multi-cheater.

"I thought you were dating me, and me alone," Susha exclaimed. Her voice showed a touch of angst, too.

Carla looked at Susha. "Who are you?"

"I'm Tim's girlfriend."

"No, I'm—" I started to say, "Tim's girlfriend," then shook my head. "Let's not start that." I stopped my head shake to glare at our problem.

Tim looked at me, then Susha, then Carla. "Ladies, I can explain." He spread his hands wide.

"So, explain and make it good," I said.

"Real good," Carla chimed in. She placed her hand on her holster.

Susha nodded in agreement.

"Well," Tim said with a wide, sexy grin, "there's plenty of me to go around. And I figure you girls are all of an age where you'd appreciate a man paying attention to you."

"You girls?" I narrowed my eyes and gritted my teeth. Why did I not see the real Tim, conniving jerk, until now?

Susha snarled. "An age? What age?"

"Appreciate?" Carla said and drew her gun. Must be a comfort move.

Tim didn't answer and didn't appear to notice our reactions. He must be real confident in his ability to schmooze women. Or stupid. Through my red haze of rage, I voted for the latter.

I thought of something. "Carla, were you going to pay for lunch?"

She nodded. "Yup, fool that I am."

The word "pay" clearly startled Tim. That sure got the gigolo's attention. "Now girls," he spread his hands wide, "it's not like you've got men coming around, not at your age. You should be grateful. You should pay me money too, not just pay for a few meals."

Susha sputtered.

Carla's mouth hung open.

And me? I had an idea. I looked at Susha and then Carla. When I had their attention, I said, "Girls," with a heavy sarcastic emphasis on the word, "if we all aim at his cheating heart and all fire on the count of three—"

"Maybe we can get rid of the body before anybody shows up," Carla finished. She knew how slow Mondays were in Open Carry.

Susha added, "Or if we get caught, we can share the blame."

Carla raised her pistol. "Let's do some straight shooting. Just like Tim taught us."

"On the count of three." I took aim. "One."

Tim raised his arms high. "Girls?"

Susha aimed. "Two."

Tim said. "This is a joke, right?" Slow learner, our Tim.

Carla grinned and aimed. "Three."

We fired straight and true.

"Wait!" Tim cried. His last word. He crumpled to the floor.

Through the ringing in my ears, I heard the front door thump open. Beyond it stood Erica with Bob right behind her.

Eyes wide, Erica said, "I got out quick from the dentist."

Dang. What a good employee.

Bob stepped in front of Erica. "And it's almost noon. Opening time," he said.

Double dang. What a good customer.

"We saw everything," Erica added.

Triple dang.

***

Eleven months later headlines claim:

Bob Richards's and Erica Maloney's Testimony at Simultaneous Scorned Shooters Trial Judged Key for Crime of Passion Defense.

Two weeks after that:

Jury Convicts Simultaneous Scorned Shooters of Manslaughter.

Three weeks later:

Jury Suggests Time Served for the Simultaneous Scorned Shooters.

Six months after that:

Triple S Bar, Once Open Carry, Opens. Simultaneous Scorned Shooters Are Joint Owners.

Today:

I looked around the gun-free Triple S bar, co-owned by Susha, Carla and me. Gone were the paintings of famous gunslingers,

90

save for Annie Oakley. In their place hung portraits of strong women: Rosa Parks, Susan B. Anthony, Marie Curie and more.

Susha set up for her session on the fireplace ledge, leaving her new acquaintance, a tall, dark, handsome stranger, sitting by himself. Carla swept in, pretending to only be taking his order, a lie shown by how she leaned over him, showing lots of crepe paper cleavage.

Not so fast, witch-with-a-b, I thought. I strode over to them, and in my sexiest voice, said "You have other tables, Carla. No worries, I'll take care of this one."

Carla huffed, hand on her hip where her holster used to be. Old habits die hard, I supposed.

The man made a small noise in the back of his throat.

Out of the corner of my eye I spotted Susha headed our way, full steaming with a big Texas mad.

Bring it, fat girl.

"I saw him first." She planted her feet wide apart, in a perfect shooter's stance.

"Yeah, and I'm certain he saw your fat behind first too," I said, pointing at the offensive body part.

There was a rustle from the man in his chair, but I didn't dare take my eyes off my two co-owners. They didn't have guns. That didn't mean they were unarmed. Susha had purple nails of steel and Carla's arm muscles from hanging her paintings—well, ooh-boy.

Carla smoothed her hand over her hip, as if searching for a missing gun. "Face it, girls, I'm the best-looking, youngest gal here, neither of you got a chance."

"I'm the one who put up the money for this bar," Susha said.

"Money already spent, that you can't get back unless this bar makes it back," Carla said.

I made a pistol out of my hand and pointed it in Carla's direction. "And I'm the one with the experience and knowledge to make this place work." My point swiveled Susha's way. "And our fame as the Simultaneous Scorned Shooters won't bring people in forever."

"You're them?" The man's voice squeaked at the end of his

question.

I swung my pretend pistol to point at the stranger. "So, shoot us."

Instead, the man jumped to his feet and fled the Triple S.

"There goes our problem," Carla said.

"Good riddance. No man is worth it," Susha said.

"Forgot that for a moment," Carla said. "Need to remember what might happen. Again."

I holstered my imaginary pistol in an imaginary holster and said, "Yup, nothin' worse than trouble in a Tucson bar."

~*~

DESERT BLOOMERS GARDENING CLUB

LYNN NICHOLAS

Her mouth was drawn in a self-righteous line. Rita detested manspeak. Who did this new club member think he was, butting in and drawing attention to himself, acting like he was the reigning authority on pruning roses? Well, not on her watch. It looked like someone was in need of a reality check.

"Excuse me for interrupting, Stanley. Do I have that right? Did you say your name is Stanley?" Rita pulled her lips into a smile, but her eyes were narrowed.

Stan stopped mid-soliloquy. A look of mild confusion furrowed his brow. "Um…yes. Stanley. Stan, is okay as well."

"Everyone." Rita stood up to ensure she had the group's attention and to reinforce her established position as club president. "For those of you who haven't met our newest member, let me introduce Mr. Stanley Parker, a new arrival to Tucson." She gestured toward Stanley, who was now standing as well, sun hat grasped in his hands. "Mr. Parker was president of his gardening club back in Snohomish, Washington, and he's ready to share his expertise with our little Desert Bloomers Gardening Club. I hope you will all extend him a warm welcome, and help him acclimate to the challenges of gardening in our Southwestern desert."

The mainly female group murmured welcomes, accompanied by nudges and not-so-subtle exchanged looks. First, Stanley was tall, trim and quite attractive, with a full head of silvering hair. Second, almost everyone at one time or another had dared to stand up to Rita, and by now, each one of them knew better. More than one member of Desert Bloomers had attempted to run against her as club president, but Rita always managed to deflate their campaigns before they got off the ground.

"Now." Rita clapped her hands. "Let's get back to the business at hand. We still have to plan our trip to Roses Galore Nursery. Our club members will get first pick of this season's new rose bushes."

Stanley sat down.

***

Stanley Parker strolled to the edge of the flagstone patio and surveyed his new backyard. The warmth from his coffee mug felt good against his arthritic hands. Even though the landscaping at his new house was incomplete, the previous owner had planted good anchor plants that he could design around.

April in Tucson was truly gorgeous. A palo verde tree, just beginning to burst into yellow bloom, took center stage in the garden. From what the realtor had shared with him, many of the delicate-looking shrubs along the back wall were indigenous, planted both to conserve water and attract butterflies. The smallish shrubs bearing pink fluff balls were called fairy dusters; the tall spikes of bright pink were penstemons, and the thick-leaved plant in the far back corner was a jimson weed, also known as devil's trumpet, or datura. The name made Stanley smile. Thanks to the realtor, he now knew jimson weed was toxic, but since he didn't have outdoor pets, he wasn't worried. Stanley was looking forward to the large, white flowers the plant would bear once the summer heat hit. Behind the jimson weed was a large, woody shrub with striking star-shaped leaves. He knew that one was a castor bean plant, also toxic. The center of the backyard sported gravel instead of a lawn, but there was plenty of room around the edges to add colorful flower beds. Stanley's tapped the side of the ceramic mug with his fingernails—tapping helped him think. His first task was to get up-to-speed with the botanical names of these arid land plants.

Back in Snohomish, Stanley had a monthly spot on a local, televised gardening show. He prided himself on being more of a horticulturist than a simple gardener. Each month he featured a new gardening technique or a special seasonal plant to add color or texture to his neighbors' gardens. He gave short presentations on everything from growing stately tulips to warnings about highly toxic plants like foxglove, also known as digitalis. The juxtaposition of beauty to toxicity fascinated him.

Stanley gulped the last of the coffee but held on to the mug; his nails tapped out a staccato beat. There would be a learning curve to gardening in this part of the Southwest, but he was never one to back down from a challenge. The Desert Bloomers Gardening Club could turn out to be an excellent resource for him. With the exception of Rita, who reminded him too much of his late wife, there was potential within the group to form some useful alliances and pick brains.

The front doorbell chimed out the synthesized tones of Westminster's Big Ben. The sound was set to an ear-splitting level. Sighing, Stanley set the coffee mug on the patio table. He wasn't expecting anyone, and this caller was persistent. The chiming was now on its second pass. He made a mental note to change the ring to a normal, unobtrusive, ding-dong.

"Hello. Uh…what can I do for you?" Stanley said to the stylish, fiftyish woman on his doorstep.

"Oh, hello. I'm sure you don't remember me." The woman's overly lip-sticked lips curved upwards as she tilted her head back to meet Stan's blue eyes. "I'm Connie McGovern. I was at the garden club meeting when Rita introduced you to the group. She mentioned that you are new to Tucson, and I thought you and your wife might enjoy a night off from cooking. I made my special green chili casserole as a way to welcome you to both the club and Tucson."

Stanley blinked twice and swallowed hard. He opened the door a bit wider and reached out to accept the casserole dish. Among his many talents, he was also an excellent cook. But, as busy as he was, a break from his own cooking was more than welcome.

"Well, thank you, um…Connie. I, ah, well, there's no wife. I'm a widower. I'm sure I will enjoy your special dish. One thing I already love about Tucson is the flavorful Mexican food."

Connie smiled and ducked her head.

Stanley stepped back from the door.

Connie edged a bit closer, as if to follow her casserole dish into the house.

Stanley began to swing the door shut. "I must get this casserole into the 'fridge. I'm sorry I can't invite you in. I'm still not completely settled, and there's not much to see in the garden as yet. Thank you, though. Very kind." He stepped backward. "I appreciate the gesture. I'm sure I'll see you at the next club meeting." He swung the door shut. As the door latch clicked, he could hear Connie say something about looking forward to seeing him again.

"Oh my," he said to himself. If history held true, this wouldn't be the first casserole to appear on his doorstep.

***

Rita's thoughts tumbled while she arranged the metal folding chairs for the garden club meeting. This morning's clear skies were rapidly disappearing under fast-moving clouds. Late June was early for a monsoon, but the low-level clouds looked threatening. Stanley had pushed for a lakeside setup, but Rita made the quick judgement call to move the meeting to a huge ramada in the same park. Stanley didn't understand about Tucson's sudden summer storms. Two folded chairs clanged together as Rita almost threw another one to the floor. She looked around to make sure an early arrival hadn't witnessed her minor temper tantrum. Rita took a deep breath and curbed the outward signs of her irritation. Her outrage, though, felt more than justified. Something had to be done about the way Stanley was bullying her. He managed to make everything he said sound like the logical voice of reason, while making her sound like she was being difficult and obstinate.

Rita had learned to guard her back long ago in her sorority days. Women can be covertly competitive. They chip away behind the scenes. It's nothing new. Women have been indoctrinated from a very young age to upend their competition, whether vying for a man's attention or wanting to reign as the prettiest of them all. It's the basis of most fairy tales, like the sadly fated Snow White. Being in competition with a man, however, required a totally different approach. They played the game out in the open with confidence, building alliances and mustering the troops. She was going to have to beat him at his own game and play on his weaknesses.

In general, Rita disliked men. A happy widow for fifteen years, she had no intention to ever marry again. Most men, she'd learned, could be diverted by placating their egos. However, it appeared that this Stanley was going to be more of a challenge. Four months into his membership, and there had been nothing but trouble for her in the garden club. Stanley was like a desert dust devil, stirring things up. To make matters worse, too many of the single ladies were halfway in love with him, bickering over where his interest might lie, and the rest of the members looked up to him as some kind of gardening guru. And darned if the man hadn't wangled his way into the Pima County Master Gardener's Program. Rita kicked another chair.

And there he was now, heading toward the ramada, radiating an air of authority, his fawning entourage at his heels. Maybe this would be the meeting where she could quietly insinuate that Stanley wasn't the great guy everyone seemed to think he was. Rita had done a little digging. Mr. Nice Guy had some skeletons rattling around in his garden shed.

"Hello, ladies. Hello, Stanley. How's everyone this lovely summer morning, despite the humidity?" Rita beamed her best "all is right with the world" face.

"Rita, nice choice of meeting space. Appreciate the shade.

Don't you agree, Stanley?" Julia said. She was practically glued to Stanley's elbow. Julia was all decked out in a waist-cincher of a sundress.

"Now Julia," Grace chimed in, "give our Stanley some breathing space."

Rita noticed that Grace's hair had recently been highlighted. Seems that a good-looking, financially secure, straight male is in high demand these days in Tucson.

"Stanley," Rita said, in a drippy-sweet tone, "I drove by your house and couldn't help but notice that all your lovely azaleas had died. They looked so very sad. Azaleas just don't grow well here. You'll learn. Tucson is anything but Washington state. I'd be happy to loan you my copy of Plants for Arid Lands." Rita finished with a teasing laugh.

Stanley bristled and jutted out his chin. "I have to say, I'm rather hurt that you would bring that up. After all, you know I'm new to desert gardening, and I know more than anyone that I still have a lot to learn." His face flushed penstemon pink.

Rita breathed in deeply.

Stanley was no slouch at winning the sympathy vote.

She stepped back and placed a palm over her heart, making sure to catch the eye of as many club members as possible. "Oh dear. I would never hurt anyone's feelings intentionally." Rita's voice quavered. "You are being overly sensitive to take offense at such a simple statement. I thought you had more of a sense of humor. And, I was merely being helpful by offering the loan of the plant book. I didn't mean to step on your toes. Goodness gracious, now you've hurt my feelings."

Rita's ability to gaslight was new only to Stanley. Julia and Grace exchanged looks. One or two other ladies bit their lips and turned away.

"Now, Rita. I didn't mean—" Stanley began. His words were cut off by her raised hand.

"I think we should just get on with the meeting," Rita said. She lifted her chin, put on her bravest but most-persecuted look, and walked behind the table in front of the group. "Let's get started, shall we?"

Everyone took their seats. Rita smiled.

***

"I'm telling you, Grace, the man is gunning for me. Don't be fooled. He's not just being helpful. He has his eye on being club president and on winning the year's best community-minded club award. Not to mention the award for the most attrative backyard landscaping."

"Rita, I think you have Stanley all wrong. He's just a very enthusiastic gardener and obliging human being. You started this club, and we all know how much work you've put into it. No one can replace you." Grace handed Rita a glass of iced tea and motioned her toward a shaded patio chair. "Stanley's idea to start a community garden at Blenman Elementary School was excellent and well-received by both the community and our club. He even has Tucson Botanical Gardens on board."

"Yes, yes, yes, it's a fine idea. It's not his ideas I object to, it's the way he presents them and the way he downplays mine." Rita took a big swallow of her iced tea. "Didn't you notice that when the reporter from KUAT did a short bit on the community garden idea, she just assumed Stanley was president of the Desert Bloomers Gardening Club. She didn't even mention my name. Then, at the happy hour at Carmen's house last week, he had the nerve to say that some of our fun little fund-raisers were comparable to 1950s bake sales, and we needed to be more innovative. I don't think the man is community-minded as much as power hungry."

"Rita, you need to take the time to really get to know him. He's fun and very interesting to talk to. Stanley loves to go out to eat, especially Mexican food. I've even taken him a few of my special dishes, as have other club members. He often invites us to sit on his patio and chat for a while."

"Geez Louise. I live alone and don't see any of you stopping by with yummy bean burritos or enchilada casseroles for me! I'll be glad to chat on the patio for free food."

"Rita, you are a gas. Really!" Grace patted Rita's hand and giggled just enough to lighten the mood.

"Well, let me tell you something I haven't told anyone else. I learned something about our Mr. Perfect Stanley Parker. Something I'm sure he doesn't want anyone here to know." Rita leaned forward and lowered her voice as if the wind or the backyard birds might eavesdrop and spread rumors.

As reluctant as she proclaimed to be about listening to gossip, Grace turned her good ear toward Rita so she wouldn't miss anything.

"I talked to a woman from the gardening club in Snohomish about cannas, and I managed to bring the subject around to Stanley. Seems that Stanley moved away to avoid some gossip that had turned nasty. What I heard was that when Stanley's wife passed away, he was not only left with a nice hunk of life insurance but some real estate holdings as well, which he slowly sold off. His business at the time was flipping houses and real estate. I also learned that he'd moved to Snohomish from Seattle, and he was also a recent a widower when he arrived in town. He met his second wife at a charity garden-society event."

"Well," Grace said, "that's more sad than suspicious, don't you think?"

"Maybe on the surface." Rita pressed her lips together and raised her eyebrows. "But, there's more. The first wife, who was older than Stanley, passed away just three years after they married. The second wife, who was also a widow and older than Stanley, didn't last too long either. Both wives died unexpectedly, and both left Stanley in very comfortable financial circumstances. But that's not all."

Rita leaned back and folded her arms.

"Okay, so go on." Grace bit her top lip but leaned forward to catch every word.

"This Chatty-Cathy I spoke with at the Snohomish club also confided that the brother of Stanley's last wife had been harassing him. The harassment had reached the point where Stanley told some of his friends that he was going to have to get a restraining order. It was over some major disagreement about his late wife's will. Sounded really ugly."

"I have to say, this is distressing to hear. I truly like Stanley." Grace's frown was more quizzical than anxious. "He really is well-liked, Rita. He's been coming out of his shell and letting people get to know him. Actually, I think that pushy Sheila Cummings invited him over for lunch tomorrow. If she had her way, she'd be wife number three and would be quite happy about it, gossip or no gossip. I heard about the invite from Connie, who was hopping mad because she wanted to ask Stanley to accompany her to an art fair tomorrow afternoon. Honestly, I hate to believe he could be hiding anything. I think our Stanley might just be the victim of some very mean-spirited gossip. He's such a charming man."

"Well, all I know is that charming man tried to blame me for losing his chance at winning a ribbon at the Pima County Iris Show. It came back to me that he thought I was the one who'd left his irises out of the cold storage all night, which ruined his exhibit. I could have spit I was so mad. If it was anyone, it was Donna, who will do anything to defend her first-place wins. But Stanley goes and blames me. I'll say it again. He's gunning for me, doesn't like me, and wants to be club president, and I just won't have it."

"Rita, you're being overly sensitive and maybe just a tad paranoid. I don't know who told you that story about the iris show, but I never heard Stanley say any such thing. Although I do know he was upset about his cut irises being left out overnight to open too soon. Any one of us would have been upset. But, in terms of what you heard about his life in Snohomish, I think we should give Stanley the benefit of the doubt."

"Keep those blinders on, Grace, and stay in your happy place. Anyway, before you take off, I have some canna rhizomes to share with you. Maybe you should share them with Stanley and, while you are there, dig around for the truth."

***

Stanley held the front window blinds open just wide enough to get a clear view of the street. Maybe he was paranoid, but it seemed like the same tan truck had been making slow passes by his house for days. He'd also seen what looked like the same truck circling the Trader's Joe's parking lot yesterday when he was loading groceries into his car. His cell phone was at the ready. He needed to get a photo of the truck's license plate number to confirm his suspicions. He didn't leave his forwarding address with anyone in Snohomish, but…. He might have to find grounds to file a new restraining order here in Arizona.

Stanley poured a double scotch, neat. He sipped as he walked through the house. He was happy here in Tucson. Things were working out. He'd found a niche in the gardening club, and he'd recently widened his social circle by hitting some golf balls at the driving range. He might even apply for an Arizona real estate license to ground himself further in the community. Stanley opened the French doors and stepped outside. The overhead fans kept the covered patio tolerable for late July. His garden was thriving. The castor bean shrub was in full bloom, and even the new cacti looked happy in their rocky bed along the west wall.

Stanley didn't want any trouble in Tucson. Besides the potential threat of harassment from his late wife's belligerent brother, his only obstacle to establishing himself here was Rita. The brother-in-law he could handle, but Rita was tougher to crack than a coconut. She had the power to upend the new life he was building. He'd heard she was fueling the flames of rumors, trying her best to poke holes in his armor. He'd cultivated a demeanor of gentlemanly graciousness, and he couldn't risk letting her provoke him into losing his temper and damaging his image.

***

Rita sat at the kitchen table staring out the patio sliders, absentmindedly stirring her tea. She'd had enough. She was done with Stanley. He'd pushed the envelope to bursting. Now he was actively running against her for president of the garden club. She couldn't let him take her identity away from her. Maybe it was time to take a different tack with this man. It was time to play at being nice and treat him to her famous, spicy pinto-bean-enchilada casserole. It was her late husband's favorite dish.

***

"I'm so pleased to get to finally see and photograph your award-winning garden design. Thank you for agreeing to do a short interview for my article in The Desert Leaf."

"You're more than welcome. I have a refreshment cart over here on the patio. Please, help yourselves, both you and your photographer. I have hot coffee, cold drinks, and some excellent fresh pastries."

"We appreciate your thoughtfulness," Joe said, adjusting his hold on the recorder to accommodate a pastry. "I know it's been a tough couple of months for all of you in the Desert Bloomers Gardening Club. I heard that you lost one of your most active members—a Stanley Parker?"

"Yes." Rita replied. She lowered her eyes and pressed her lips together. "We were all so very fond of Stanley. His passing was a great shock."

"Again, my condolences. But, that said, I want to extend congratulations for being elected the club president. This is your eighth consecutive year as president, is that correct?"

"Thank you. Yes. I started the club just over eight years ago. It's been a bittersweet win. Stanley was hoping to run against me. The challenge would have been fun, but we're a strong group and the club members have all rallied."

"Wonderful." Joe signaled to his photographer to follow him. "I love how you've incorporated both colorful bedding plants and indigenous plants into the garden. Your design was praised for the inclusion of so many plants for pollinators."

Rita let Joe go at his own pace as he directed his photographer.

"Rita, is that large shrub with the white flowers a castor bean?"

"Yes. My late husband planted it about twenty years ago."

"They are such striking plants, but they are so poisonous. I can't have a castor bean plant in my yard because of my dogs. Oh...you might find this tidbit interesting. A toxicologist I recently

103

interviewed at Tucson Botanical Gardens said that the castor bean seed looks exactly like a pinto bean. Did you know that?" Joe stopped mid-stride, recorder in hand.

"You know," Rita said, a bemused frown forming on her brow, "with everything I know about desert plants, I somehow missed that interesting bit of information." She shook her head. "I guess I'll have to be careful not to mix them up." Rita trilled her most charming laugh. "Now, let's walk over this way so I can show off my cannas. The blooms are drop-dead gorgeous this year."

A PAGE FROM THE PAST

JEFFREY J. MARIOTTE

Being perp-walked in handcuffs cross the University of Arizona campus during the Tucson Festival of Books with about 90,000 people watching, at least 15% percent of them recording it on their phones, might not have been the most embarrassing moment of Dave Tanner's life, but for sure it was in the top five.

Tanner loved the festival. He wasn't in the business, but he had a friend named Norman Pope who had a vast collection of science fiction and mystery books going back to the 1930s. They filled room after room of his Foothills home, which had been left to him by parents who'd had more practical ideas about making a living than Norman did. Norman was good at spending the stuff, but considerably less skilled at earning it. The trust he was left took care of his financial needs and the house was paid off before his parents passed, so Norman had spent the first sixty-five years of his life acquiring his collection. Suddenly, in his sixty-sixth year, he had realized that he had no heirs and wasn't likely to produce any at that point, so he decided to start selling off the books little by little. Some—his favorite four or five hundred, he would keep until the bitter end, but the rest he would try to place in good homes where they would be as loved as they had been with him.

Every year, he took a booth at the Tucson Festival of Books. Every year, Tanner helped him pack up and load in and unpack and set up, then hung around the booth and helped keep track of sales, spelled Norman for his frequent bathroom breaks, ran to the food court for lunches and drinks, and occasionally stole away to do some browsing of his own or to attend an interesting panel or three. The festival was not primarily oriented toward old or used books; most of the booths were taken by publishers or special-interest groups or self-published authors. But the scarcity of antiquarian booksellers, mixed with the quality of Norman's collection, meant he had fairly steady traffic all weekend. Some were regular customers who came back with their want lists every year, and others were people who just happened by and recognized treasures when they saw them.

Saturday had been busy. Norman, seventy-three now, could barely keep up, so Tanner had busied himself sprucing up the bookshelves and tables after browsers—some tornado-like in their fervor—swept through. Today, Sunday, was a little quieter, and Tanner was sitting in a chair at the edge of the booth. Fortunately, Norman had been clever enough to acquire an end booth near the UA Mall Tent, open to the north and east, which meant the hot afternoon sun didn't blaze in. The booth had the aroma of old paper, which made it smell like Norman's home until a breeze wafted through.

"You take good care of that one," Norman said to a customer walking away with a first edition hardcover of James M. Cain's The Postman Always Rings Twice. "And if you figure out who the hell the postman is, call me and let me know!"

"Will do," the customer promised. He wasn't much younger than Norman. Then again, neither was Tanner. The phrase "antiquarian bookseller" had a double meaning, because most of the people who sold antiquarian books were antiques themselves, as were many of their patrons.

"Ahh, Dave," Norman said when the buyer had left, "I hate to see that one go."

"Why'd you sell it, then? I mean, besides the two thousand bucks you just pocketed."

"I can't hold on to everything forever. Besides, I've still got a few copies back home. The Vintage paperback, the Pocket Books

from '47 and '53, the Grosset and Dunlap Photoplay edition—"
He let the sentence trail off.

"You think you're going to read it again?" Tanner asked.
"Ever?"

Norman's broad shoulders pushed toward his neck, the closest
he could get to a shrug. He had always been a big man, beefy—he
had been a member of the Society for Creative Anachronism, and
always played a royal because nobody could accept a peasant or
even a knight who was so well-fed. "You never know. It ain't long,
don't take more than a day if you set your mind to it."

Tanner thought it would be rude to point out that at this
moment, Norman probably still owned more books than he had
days remaining. What Norman didn't have a lot of were friends,
so when he did go, it would probably fall to Tanner to dispose of
the rest of the collection.

The booth was quiet for a few moments, both men lost in
their own thoughts. Then a young woman wandered in, her gaze
seemingly caught by the unusual sight of old books, most with
dust jackets protected in archival sleeves.

"G'morning, missy," Norman said. "What do you like to
read?"

She looked at him, smiled. She might have been a student
at the college. Tanner was pretty good at guessing ages—one
of several habits left over from a decade-long stint at the San
Francisco PD, but he couldn't quite pin her down. Anywhere
between eighteen and twenty-eight, he guessed. Her T-shirt and
leggings had both seen better days. She was slender, with dark
skin, straight but lustrous black hair, and big eyes that were almost
as black as her hair. She might have been Latina, but then again,
she might not have been. When she spoke, though, her accent
was pure Arizona.

"A little bit of everything, I guess."

"You're in luck," Norman said. "That's what we got!"

She grinned, a smile that seemed to illuminate the
shadowed interior of the booth. She was pretty, and probably
used to old men trying in vain to flirt with her. She scanned the
standing bookcases—science fiction and fantasy against the left

107

wall, mystery and noir against the right. In between, as a kind of transition zone, stood a table displaying the works of some authors who had toiled in all those fields.

When she got to the table, she stopped. "Oh, you have Bradbury," she said. "He was my mom's favorite. Mine, too."

"He's about as good as it gets," Norman said. He might say that about any author a potential buyer mentioned, but in this case, he meant it.

The young woman traced the spines lightly with her fingertips, then paused them on a copy of the thick collection called The Stories of Ray Bradbury. "Ooh," she said.

"Take a look," Norman said. "Great collection."

She pulled it gently from its row on the table, turned it over and scanned the back, then opened it. "It's autographed!"

"Twice," Norman said. "Signed on the title page, and there's an inscription on page four-hundred-sixty-nine. Fellow I acquired it from didn't know the meaning of that inscription. I knew Ray for a good number of years, but never thought to ask him. Miss him like hell. Excuse my French."

She nodded, her attention riveted on the book. She turned to a page near the back—469, Tanner guessed—and her eyes grew about as wide as a full moon just clearing the horizon. Then she shook her head and started to return it to its spot on the table. "Thank you," she said.

As she turned away, she slipped, or seemed to, and caught herself on the books. But in so doing, she shoved the front row toward the back, pushing a half-dozen of the books in the back row off the table and onto Norman's lap. "Oh, I'm so sorry!" she cried. Trying to correct herself, she knocked a few books from the front row off, and they landed in the grass under the table.

Tanner left his seat to pick them up, and as he did, she spun around and broke into a sprint.

Tanner turned to watch her go—and realized she had The Stories of Ray Bradbury clutched in her hand.

"Norm, she's got the book!" he shouted.

Norman was still juggling the books she had shoved onto him, trying to get them back on the table without tweaking dust jackets or soiling page blocks. Tanner snatched up the ones that had hit the grass and plopped them onto the table. "I'll be back."

He could just see the top or her head, mostly because of the way people moved to one side or another to avoid her headlong dash. He doubted they'd be so considerate as to do the same for a gray-haired, sixty-five-year-old man, but he stayed fit and he outweighed the woman by probably a hundred pounds, so they might regret it if they didn't.

He raced after her, barreling through the gap she had cut through the crowded walkway. As the opening started to close, he shouted "Coming through!" Those who heard got out of the way. Some didn't, and Tanner tried to sidestep them, but shouldered one man who was so deep into what he was saying to an obviously bored companion that he couldn't be bothered. The impact caused the man to stagger, and he shouted some choice profanities at Tanner's retreating back.

Tanner wanted to scream "Stop! Thief!" like they did in the comics, but he didn't figure today's youngsters would get it. They might stop where they were—in his way—or think he was the thief. Subtlety, he feared, was a vanishing tradition. Instead, he charged forward, occasionally crying "Out of the way!" Because she was shorter than many people, he lost track of her a couple of times, but he spotted her again when she hung a right on Cherry Ave. He scanned for a shortcut, saw none because of other booths in the way, and followed. When he got to the walkway's intersection with Cherry, she was swinging left on the southern walkway. He had gained on her, but he wasn't there yet.

Instead of following, he continued on the northern walkway, then cut down through the relatively open space between the area called the Circus and Science City, bellowing as he did so, because this was a children's zone and kids were even worse at dodging sprinting adults than other adults were. When he reached the other walkway, he had closed the gap.

He was so focused on watching the young woman move through the crowd that he almost didn't notice the two men in blue coming toward him. "Hold it!" one of them shouted.

Tanner ignored the command and bulled forward into a solid

wall of blue. Someone grabbed his arm and growled, "I said hold it."

There were two of them, both bigger than Tanner, and younger, glaring at him with that look that Tanner had perfected ages ago on the streets of San Francisco. Over one cop's shoulder, he saw the thief disappearing into the crowd. "You don't understand, officers," he said.

"What's to understand? You're presenting a hazard to yourself and others, especially those kids you almost ran over."

"I was chasing a thief. Look, I was on the job for ten years. I'm a licensed PI in Arizona. I can show you my license, but you're letting her get away with a valuable book."

"File a report," the cop said. His breath smelled minty, and he had a wad of gum in his mouth. He was a white guy with a shaved head, and he wore wraparound sunglasses against the brightness. The other officer was black and looked bored with the whole thing.

Tanner was out of luck. The Bradbury book was gone. "I'm reaching for my wallet," he said. "I'm not armed." With exaggerated motions, he moved his right hand behind his back, plucked his wallet from his jeans and withdrew the license. He handed it to the bald cop, while the other studied him as if he were an alien species.

Maybe he was. He was wearing a sky-blue denim shirt with pearl snaps, with the top three open and wisps of white chest hair showing beneath a silver man-in-the-maze pendant on a leather thong, given to him by a Tohono O'odham friend. His sleeves were rolled up, and his left wrist sported three leather-and-silver bracelets. He wore faded blue jeans with western boots on his feet. His silver hair curled up around his ears, and he had the deep tan of the desert-dweller that he was. If he had ever looked like a cop, he didn't now.

The bald cop nodded and handed back the license. "Looks legit," he said. "You said something about a stolen book?"

"I'm here working a booth with a friend of mine. He's got a lot of very valuable books, so I help out and provide security at the same time. This woman snatched one from the table and ran for it. I gave chase."

"Show us the booth," the cop said.

"Sure." Tanner started to turn around, but then the other cop grabbed his arm and wrenched it behind his back.

"Can't take a chance on you running or trying anything."

"You're really going to cuff me?"

"If you'd rather, we can just put you in a patrol car and take you to booking."

Tanner didn't have to think about it. "Cuff me."

The cop made them tight, but not painfully so. Professional courtesy, Tanner figured. Still, he was a spectacle, being led through most of the festival's grounds by a pair of cops, his hands obviously cuffed behind his back. The only people who didn't stare were those who didn't notice. And even with so much else to look at, there seemed to be precious few of those.

When they finally reached Norman's booth, he broke out laughing. "So the law finally caught up to you," he said between wheezy eruptions.

"That's not funny," Tanner said. "Well, maybe a little. But tell 'em what happened so they'll take these bracelets off me."

Norman eyed him carefully for a moment, then said, "Never seen this guy before in my life."

Tanner felt one of the officers grab the handcuffs, as if he might try to escape. "Come on, Norman."

"I'm kidding, I'm kidding," he told the cops. "Yes, he works with me here. Some girl swiped a Ray Bradbury and he took off after her." Fixing his gaze back on Tanner, he added, "Appears you didn't catch her."

"I would've, if not for these guys."

"All right," the bald cop said. Tanner heard him unlock the cuffs and free his wrists. He brought them around, massaged them. "I guess you're okay. Just don't go causing a commotion and scaring little kids, or we'll have a problem."

"You have my word," Tanner said.

The officers left.

Tanner considered giving Norman a hard time for denying their friendship, but decided it wasn't worth it. He was the best friend Norman had, but Norman loved a good joke or a good book more than he did any mere human being.

Tanner sat down in his regular spot. "Sorry about the book, Norm."

"It's okay. It's just one book."

"Sounds like a unique copy."

"Oh, it is. But Ray loved meeting readers and signing books, so there are a lot of his out there."

That didn't sit well with Tanner. Sure, Norman had more books than he could ever dispose of, and he didn't want for money. Maybe it was Tanner's years in law enforcement, but the idea that somebody—in the midst of a festival held to honor books—would just run off with one continued to disturb him.

Then he had another thought. "You know what? Let me check something out."

"If that's a euphemism for going to the toilet, you can just say it right out."

"It's not," Tanner said, rising from the chair. "I'll be back in a bit."

Leaving the festival grounds, he cut across the loop surrounding Old Main and tried the Douglass Building first. Not finding her there, he crossed University Boulevard to the Arizona State Museum. She wasn't outside. It was possible that she'd gone in, but she would have to pay eight bucks for that, unless she was a UA student with a Cat card. He could check in there later, but first he headed past Old Main again and through part of the festival.

He found her sitting on a bench outside the Main Library, reading the Bradbury book. She probably didn't know that this library had only been built in 1977, and that in earlier days the university's library had been housed in Douglass and in the Arizona State Museum building. Hanging out with Norman, you learned that kind of thing.

Focused on the book, she didn't see Tanner until he sat beside her and put a hand on her shoulder. It was a friendly touch, but firm enough that he could grasp her if she tried to bolt.

"Oh!"

"Yeah," he said. "Oh."

"Look, I'm really sorry," she said. "I shouldn't have done that."

"No, you shouldn't."

"But . . . the thing is, it's my book. I mean, it's supposed to be my book. Was, anyway."

"Yours, how?"

She met his gaze for a moment, her brown eyes huge and liquid. "It was my mom's. She told me all about it when I was little. When she was . . . when she was here. She loved Ray Bradbury's writing. She never had much money or anything, but she had some of his paperbacks around our place—even when we lived in her car, she kept them. And she always told me about how he had come to Tucson one day when she was pregnant. She went to hear him speak, and she bought this book and had it signed. She asked him to sign it for me, even though I wasn't born yet, and to do it on the page that her favorite story was on."

"Let me guess," Tanner said. "Four-hundred-sixty-nine?"

"That's right." She flipped through pages and stopped on that one. It was the first page of a story called "Dark They Were, and Golden-Eyed." Above the title, Bradbury had written "For Cora, in the future!" and signed his name beneath it.

"I'm Cora," she said. "Named after the wife in the story."

"And he signed this book for you before you were born."

"That's why it's 'in the future.'"

"I get it," Tanner said. "But why does Norman have the book now? Why didn't she keep it?"

"Like I said, we never had much. My father abandoned her as soon as he found out she was pregnant. We lived in a trailer, or in her car, or on the streets for a little while. During one low time, when we were both hungry and there was nothing coming in, she found out that the book was more valuable with his autograph in it than what she had paid for it, so she sold it to this used bookstore on Fourth Avenue. She said it bought us a few meals. I was still so young, I had no idea how special it was or anything, so it wasn't until later that I realized what she had sacrificed."

"So when you saw it today, with that inscription in it—"

"Yeah. I knew I couldn't afford two hundred and fifty bucks. I mean, I get by, but just barely. But I'm not trying to feed a kid, right? Still, that's way too much for me to spend on a book. But I felt like I had to have it. I don't usually steal, I promise."

"I believe you," Tanner said. Every word of her story was convincing, and the way she told it, fighting to keep emotion out of her voice, didn't sound like a scam.

"Once you weren't chasing me anymore, I came here, because my mom always told me that he had lived in Tucson when he was young, and he loved this building."

"I've heard that, too," Tanner said. "That he loved the university library, and read in there constantly. I guess it was open to the public then. But it wasn't in this building at the time. I can show you where it was."

"But, I mean . . . aren't you gonna have me arrested or something? For stealing?"

Tanner shook his head. "This book wanted to be with you. Norman will understand. If he doesn't, I'll buy it, but I'm sure he will. It's yours, Cora. Try to hang onto it." He slipped his card from his wallet, folded two twenties under it, and said, "Here, this is me. If you ever need anything—anything at all—get in touch. I live in a trailer, too, though in my case it's by choice. But I get it. I'm available for whatever you might need."

She took the card, felt the bills under it, and looked at them. "Oh, I can't take—"

"You might see another book you want," he said. "It's okay, take it."

She smiled again, and he remembered how that smile had seemed to light up the interior of Norman's tent. She glanced at the card and said, "Thank you, Mr. Tanner."

"Dave."

"Dave."

"Come on, Cora," he said. He got to his feet and held out a hand to help her up. "You want to see those other library buildings? The ones Bradbury would have visited?"

"Oh, I do. I absolutely do."

He led her away from the library and back into the throngs.

114

"This festival's pretty cool, isn't it? Lot of book lovers here."

"My kind of people," Cora said.

"Mine, too," Tanner said. The glorious sunshine felt good on his skin, a gentle breeze kept the heat down, and he was walking across this beautiful campus in his favorite city with a living connection to a brilliant author, and in every direction, he saw books.

If life could get any better, he didn't know how.

~*~

ADAM CARMONA AND THE CASE OF THE SAGUARO RIPPER

JANET ALCORN

On a bright January morning, Detective Adam Carmona of the Tucson PD exited his unmarked SUV and surveyed the latest scene. Another killing, the sixth in as many months.

"Detective Carmona," one of the uniforms inside the cordon of tape called. "The vic is—"

Carmona held up a hand and the officer fell silent. She must have been new to working a Carmona crime scene, otherwise she'd have known he liked to approach his scenes fresh, cataloging details uncolored by the observations of others.

He picked at the Band-Aid on his finger and proceeded to catalog: remote desert area, a few hundred yards off a dirt road outside Ironwood Forest. The first two in this string of serial murders had been just inside the city limits, which was how Carmona had gotten involved. Now he was the head of a joint task force with the Pima County Sheriff's Department, trying to catch the most prolific serial killer in Tucson history. And failing.

A team of crime scene techs in Tyvek suits crawled over the scene, but he already knew what they'd find. Tracks from tires manufactured by the millions. Female victim with a vertical slash from sternum to pubis made with a razor knife. Death by exsanguination. No signs of sexual assault but recent intercourse with a condom. Whatever else the Saguaro Ripper was—and Carmona hated the tabloid name the press had bestowed on their unsub—he was consistent.

He was also careful. His scenes were so clean, except for the gore, that Locard himself couldn't find anything incriminating.

After getting cleared by the crime scene techs, Carmona ducked under the tape and approached to within thirty feet of the body. The victim straddled the arm of a saguaro a few feet off the ground, bound to the cactus with rope. Dark patch on abdomen, dark puddle in dirt below. White. Petite. A lock of wavy brown hair trailing over one shoulder. Something about that lock of hair looked—

A retching sound distracted him. A few more puking noises, then a young female officer emerged from behind a creosote bush and nearly stumbled into a teddy bear cholla. She was the officer who'd tried to tell him about the victim.

Carmona grabbed her arm and steadied her. "Careful, Officer. You've picked up a hitchhiker." He pointed to a cholla ball its inch-long spines embedded in the knee of her uniform pants. "Let me get my gloves." He unclipped a pair of tactical gloves from his belt, slipped them on, and removed the ball, tossing it under the cactus with a mass of its fellows.

The officer looked up at Carmona, and her freckled face flushed. "I'm sorry, Detective, I…"

Carmona checked her name badge. M. Grimes. "Officer Grimes, is this your first homicide?"

She wiped a smear of puke off a purple smartwatch like the one his wife wore. A stab of guilt pierced his chest at thought of Vickie.

"No, sir, I worked a gang shooting last week, but—"

"It wasn't like this."

"No."

"Well, I can't promise you this is the worst you'll ever see, but it'll probably make the top five. And for what it's worth, I puked at my first homicide, and it wasn't nearly this gory."

She met his eyes then and gave him a small smile. "Thanks, Detective."

A car door slammed behind him, and Detective Wyatt Bentley of the Pima County Sheriff's Department stepped under the tape, what was left of his mostly-gray hair looking like it'd been combed by a dust devil. He disregarded Grimes and addressed Carmona. "Mornin' Junior. Another one, huh? Which one this time, a hooker or a runaway?"

"She's a person." Carmona ignored the Junior. Bentley had never gotten over Carmona being chosen to lead the task force when most of the murders had been committed outside the city limits. "Officer Grimes will brief us after I take a closer look at the scene." He turned his back on Bentley and started toward the body. Grimes followed.

The victim was clothed like the others. Her khaki pants sagged below the gash in her belly, her tan sweater bunched above it, its wide neck baring half her shoul—

He froze, then willed himself to look closer. To examine the blue butterfly tattoo just visible at the neck of her shirt.

Oh, Lord, no.

Grimes said, "We found the victim's purse and ID. Her name is—"

"Dana Dorn," Carmona finished. Then he turned aside and puked on a brittlebush.

***

Lieutenant Tameka Silva, head of the Tucson PD's Violent Crimes Section, ushered Carmona and Bentley into a conference room at the County Sheriff's Tucson Mountain District Office. She and Bentley sat on one side of the table, Carmona on the other.

Silva regarded him with a mix of sternness and sympathy. "Adam, tell me how you knew Ms. Dorn."

Sweat stippled Carmona's neck, and for the first time in his seventeen-year career as a peace officer, he considered lying. "We were friends in high school. We got reacquainted on MySocial a few years ago."

Every detail matters in an investigation. How many times had he said that—to uniforms, to fellow detectives, even to his superiors? He swallowed hard and added, "We've been messaging each other pretty regularly, and some of those messages were…a little more than friendly."

She blinked.

Bentley laughed. "Detective Adam Carmona, the good church boy, busted for stepping out on his perfect little Stepford Wife. Weren't you an Eagle Scout too?"

Carmona froze, breathing deliberately and silently through his nose.

Silva said, "We'll need to see those chats."

He pulled his phone from his back pocket, typed in the security code, opened MySocial, and handed her the phone.

She set it on the table without looking at it. "Did you ever meet Ms. Dorn in person?"

"No. I haven't seen her in person since high school."

Bentley picked up the phone and started scrolling. "You sure about that?"

"Yes." Carmona braced himself for the blow he knew was coming. It came quickly.

Silva said, "I have to take you off the task force. Since Bentley's been involved with the case from the beginning, he'll replace you."

"I understand."

"And I'm putting you on administrative leave."

"Why?" The word escaped before Carmona could stop it.

She sighed. "How do you think it will look if the press finds out about these texts? They'll never believe it's a coincidence that the head of the task force had a…" She hesitated. "Personal relationship with one of the victims. You can't be anywhere near this case if that happens, and the best way to keep you out of it is to send you home."

His guts turned leaden. Of course it wasn't a coincidence. "I think Dana was targeted because of me. Every other victim was a runaway or—" He hesitated, "Another easy target. Now he breaks his pattern and just happens to choose a victim I... know?"

Silva stood. "That's certainly an angle we have to consider. Now go home, Adam. Get some rest, spend some time with Vickie. We've got this."

***

2 days later

Vickie Carmona tapped the end call button on her burner phone, tucked a blonde curl behind her ear, and smiled at the screen. Nick Harris was back in town and waiting for her at the Dry Springs Motel. They'd had some good times at the Dry Springs in the few months they'd been seeing each other. Vickie was reliving one of those times in graphic detail when her husband's heavy tread thudded down the hall from his back bedroom office. She tucked the phone into her purse and tossed the purse on the bed next to her laptop.

"How's your research going?" No matter that he wasn't supposed to be working on the Ripper case. He still spent sixteen hours a day holed up in his office.

He ran a hand through his crew cut. It'd been thick and black when they'd started dating. Now it was thinning with patches of gray at the temples. "It's coming along. I've been searching newspaper databases. Found some similar strings of killings in other cities."

"That's good." She should ask him more about what he'd found, show some interest in his work, but Nick was waiting for her.

"I need to take a break, and I know I've been neglecting you. Let's go out to dinner."

Crap. He never took breaks while he worked a case, so she had no cover story. She made one up on the fly. "I can't. I'm taking a yoga class at the gym with Elisa, and we're grabbing dinner afterward."

"You can't cancel? I've hardly seen you in what feels like

121

months."

"It's been months." The words came out flat, emotionless. She'd stopped feeling bitter years ago. Why waste the energy?

"I'm sorry. Really, Vickie, I'm sorry, but this case—"

"I know." She knew he'd sacrifice anything for other people's lives. Even her. Especially her.

"Then let's go out tonight. I can't make it up to you, I know that, but—"

"No. I have plans, and I'm not changing them." She picked up her purse and called, "Don't wait up," over her shoulder as she left their bedroom.

***

Carmona stood at his front window as his wife's white Honda rolled down the driveway. He'd expected her to be thrilled to have him home, to want to spend time with him. He could predict how suspects would react in an interrogation, but his wife of fourteen years was a mystery. Of course, he paid attention to suspects, noted every fidget, every eye twitch. He couldn't remember the last time he'd paid attention to Vickie.

But you paid attention to Dana Dorn. And now she's dead.

He sank onto the couch and scrubbed his face with his palms. He'd sacrificed his marriage for his job, and now his job and his lack of self-control had cost a woman her life. He closed his eyes and tried to pray, but the words wouldn't come. All that came were images of Dana's bled-out body.

He stood, strode down the hall to his office, and scanned the headlines of the articles he'd printed from the public library's newspaper database.

Municipal Court Judge Arrested for Serial Murders

Mayor Convicted of String of Killings

Prominent St. Louis Doctor Found Guilty of Slayings

Three different cities. Three different serial doers. Three different causes of death. In Portland the killer strangled his victims, in Minneapolis he shot them, in Sacramento he bludgeoned them. But in every case, the bodies were left in natural areas in and around the city—forests, riverbanks, state parks. And in every case, the victims were runaways or prostitutes, except for the final one. She was the wife or daughter of a prominent citizen who was eventually convicted of the crimes.

His cell phone buzzed. The screen read, No Caller ID. "This is Adam Carmona."

"We need to have a chat." Bentley sounded both stern and—was Carmona imagining it?—a little amused.

"Yes, we do. I found some cases in other cities."

"I need to ask you some more questions about Ms. Dorn. Be here in thirty minutes." Bentley hung up.

Carmona stared at the screen mouth open. Had Bentley really just ordered him in for questioning?

***

Carmona arrived at the Mountain District Office in exactly thirty minutes and was sent to wait in the same conference room where he'd been put on leave two days prior. While he waited for Bentley, he read through the stack of articles he'd printed. Nearly forty minutes later, Bentley strode in and slapped a manila folder on the table across from Carmona. "Your blood was found at the scene."

"What the—? That's not possible."

Bentley flopped into a chair across from Carmona and tapped the folder in front of him. "Says so right here. A smear of your blood was found on the rope binding Ms. Dorn. Right by the knot."

Carmona reached for the folder, but Bentley slid it away. "You had a Band-Aid on your finger when you were at the scene. Did she fight back, Adam? Or did you stab your finger on that cactus while you were tying—"

"Read these." Carmona shoved the stack of articles across the table. "I think this guy is framing me. He's done it before."

"Did she threaten to tell your wife, so you thought you'd do her like the other ones? Or maybe—"

Carmona kicked away from the table hard enough to slam the wheeled office chair into the wall behind him. Then he stood and left the conference room.

***

Back in his home office, Carmona hunched over his computer and pictured a new headline in the newspaper database:

Prominent Tucson Homicide Detective Convicted of Serial Killings

Then he studied the nearly-healed puncture on his middle finger. It'd been skewered by a sharp bit of metal under the driver's side door handle of his car when he and Vickie left for church Sunday morning. The killer must have planted something Saturday night—a piece of wire, maybe?—retrieved it during the service, and transferred his blood to the rope. His driveway was on the left side of the house, putting the driver's side door out of range of his porch camera, and his Sunday morning routine was as predictable as Arizona sunshine.

And the department had his DNA from the first Ripper killing. It'd been over 110 degrees the afternoon he'd worked that scene. His sweat had dripped on the body, so he'd given a sample so his DNA could be eliminated.

But Bentley needed more than a little blood to get an arrest warrant. What other evidence had the killer planted? Carmona had no alibis for the killings because they all happened at night when he was home and his only witness—Vickie—was asleep.

Vickie. She'd need to know what to do if, however unlikely, Bentley had him picked up before she got home. He grabbed his phone and called her.

Two rings.

Three.

Four.

After six rings, voicemail. Weird. Vickie always answered when he called. He left a message, telling her in as few words as possible what he'd learned, then ended with, "If I'm not here when you get home, call Marty Longworth." He hung up and called Longworth—the best defense attorney in Tucson—himself and left a message with his secretary.

When he'd finished, he printed the articles he'd found to PDF, typed up a short document explaining his theory, and emailed all of that to Longworth's office.

Then he texted Vickie. Emergency. Call ASAP.

***

After showering, Vickie wriggled into her jeans and long-sleeved T-shirt and redid her makeup in the bathroom mirror of their room at the Dry Springs. Nick, already dressed, sprawled across the tangled sheets. He was skinny, a little nerdy, attentive, and fun with a mop of red-brown hair and round cheeks that made him look as uncomplicated as a child. In other words, he was Adam's opposite.

She'd loved Adam once. She'd traded her purity ring for a wedding ring when she was twenty and moved from her father's authority to her husband's. Her parents' theology held no space for a girl to become her own person, because she wasn't her own person. She was an accessory.

She was Nick's accessory too, his side piece. God, she hated that phrase. It made her sound like an end table. But she thought as she stuffed her makeup bag in her purse, at least she was a well-laid table.

Nick stood and slipped on his windbreaker. "Ready to go?"

"Sure."

They walked out to his Jeep. She tossed her purse on the front floorboard, and Nick started the engine and turned up the A/C. He lowered his window to vent the accumulated heat.

"Wanna take a drive in the hills and watch the sunset?"

She checked her wrist, but her watch was in her purse where she'd stowed it before showering. "I wish I could, but Adam's home. I told him I was having dinner with a friend and going to yoga."

"Yoga, huh? Let me guess. Your favorite pose is downward facing doggie style."

She giggled. "I can think of a few others I like too. Now drive me back to my car before Adam sends half the force out looking for me." Not that he would, but she'd still parked two blocks away at Chuck's Diner. It wouldn't do for one of Adam's cop friends to see her car at a sleazy motel.

She pulled her phone from her purse. "Oh, crap. A missed call from Adam and an emergency text." She tapped Adam's name on the screen.

The Jeep jerked to a stop, and something hard dug into her side. "Give me the phone."

She stared, dazed, at the pistol barrel pressed against her ribs.

Adam picked up. "Vickie, thank goodness, I need—"

Nick snatched the phone, ended the call, and flung the phone out the window. Then he smashed the butt of the gun into the side of her head, and she blacked out.

***

Carmona tried Vickie again. He'd called twice in the five minutes since she'd called and hung up. This call went to voicemail just like the others.

To have something to do, he scanned the articles again and added pertinent details to the whiteboard in his home office. Bodies left in natural areas. Final victim the accused killer's daughter or wife.

No girlfriends or mistresses. No online flirt partners. Daughters.

Or wives.

He called Vickie again. Six rings. Voicemail.

When he'd asked Vickie to activate her phone's tracking app, he'd insisted it was only for her safety. He'd promised never to spy on her, and he'd kept that promise. But something was wrong. Even if she'd dialed him accidentally, that meant she had her phone on her. She would've seen his emergency text. Would've answered when he called.

He logged into the tracking website, selected Vickie's phone, and clicked Find. A phone icon appeared on a map of east Tucson, one block southwest of Houghton and Speedway, in front of a L-shaped building labeled Dry Springs Motel.

No wonder she wasn't answering. Looked like the only thing in danger was his marriage.

Still, better make sure, especially since the motel was at the edge of town near the kind of remote desert area where the Ripper's victims had been found.

He called her again. Hung up after three rings.

He launched the Tucson PD VPN and entered his credentials. Had they cut off his computer access?

They hadn't. He clicked into the staff directory, found Grimes' cell number, and called her.

***

Vickie's head throbbed, and when she moved it, she nearly barfed. She tried to raise her hand to the side of her head, but her hands were cuffed in front of her. She shifted. Her feet were shackled. She blinked a few times, and her eyes focused. So did her brain. Sort of.

A bump jarred her, sending a spike of pain through her head. Car. She was in a moving car. She twisted onto her side. A window with near-darkness beyond. The back of a Jeep.

Nick's Jeep.

She strained to remember but could retrieve only flashes. Sex in the motel room. Calling Adam.

A gun barrel in her ribs.

Panic ripped through her, and she kicked her bound feet against the hatch.

"You're finally awake." Nick's voice. Calm, friendly. "I thought maybe I'd hit you too hard."

"What the—"

"What the fuck am I doing? What the fuck is wrong with me?" He laughed, and the sound sent ice shards down her spine. "Have you ever said 'fuck' in your entire life?"

She didn't say it. Instead, she just said, "Why?"

"Well, now, that's a good question. Two questions, really. 'Why do I do this?' and 'Why am I doing this to you?' The first one's easy. I like it. I like it a lot."

Still calm, like he was talking about liking Italian food.

"As for the second question, well, it's not really about you. It's about your husband, the great Adam Carmona, youngest guy to make detective in forty years, head of the Saguaro Ripper Task Force, blah, blah, blah."

"Why do you care so much about Adam? Are you jeal—"

"I'm not jealous, idiot. I'm the Saguaro Ripper."

***

Twenty minutes after Carmona called Grimes and explained the situation, she called him back. "Was your wife's phone case pink with silver stars on the back?"

His stomach squirmed. "Yes."

"I found it under some shrubbery at the edge of the Dry Springs Motel lot. Unless she was crawling around under there, she didn't drop it."

His breath gusted out like he'd been sucker-punched. He dragged in enough air to speak. "Was her car in the lot?"

"No. I'll check other lots in the area. I asked the clerk in the office if he'd seen her, showed him the picture you texted me. He hadn't, and he wouldn't show me his guest records without a warrant. He doesn't have security cameras."

"Thanks. I'm on my way."

***

"So yeah," Nick continued as though he hadn't just

announced he was an infamous serial killer, "It isn't about you. It isn't really about any of the women I kill. Don't get me wrong, I like the killing part. But my favorite part is what happens to the men. The husbands, the fathers. What I do breaks them. Rich, smart, powerful, doesn't matter. They can't save the women they love, and it destroys them."

"Adam will catch you. If you kill me, he won't stop till—"

"Bzzzt. Nope. Adam"—he exaggerated the name like a schoolyard bully—"should already be a suspect in the murder of his side piece."

What the... "Adam never had—"

"Sure he did. Online only, but if I hadn't killed her, they'd have ended up doing the downward doggie style eventually. Anyway, like I was saying, he'll be suspected of that killing, but your death will seal the deal. Your phone at a seedy motel, a burner phone with our texts in your purse. I can picture the headline now: Top Detective Snaps, Kills Girlfriend and Cheating Wife. Goodbye, Detective Adam Carmona of the Tucson PD."

The Jeep slowed and turned right. Vickie braced her feet to keep from rolling. The vehicle bounced and rattled, and a cloud of dust bloomed in the rear window.

***

Carmona grabbed the Beretta he'd inherited from his father, headed for the front door, then stopped. The killer had a thirty-minute head start, maybe more. And Carmona had no idea where he was headed. He could take any one of several dirt roads that crisscrossed the desert east of Tucson.

He leaned his head against the living room wall. Think. Where would the killer go?

But he couldn't think because his brain kept serving up the same highlight reel. Dana's bled-out body. Grimes wiping puke off her watch. Vickie's body in place of Dana's, gutted and bleeding.

The watch.

Carmona yanked his phone from his pants pocket and called

Grimes. "Your watch. What kind is it?"

A pause, then, "It's a WellWatch 5."

"Does it have a GPS tracker?"

"Yes."

He hung up, dashed into the bedroom, and grabbed Vickie's laptop. He opened the WellWatch website. A thumbnail photo of his wife stared back at him from the upper-right corner of the screen. Thank goodness, she was logged in.

A few clicks, and a green dot pulsated from the center of a map. He zoomed in. A dirt road, twelve miles northeast of Saguaro National Park's east unit. Twenty miles away. In an isolated desert area.

***

The Jeep stopped, and Vickie drew her knees up, ready to kick the crap out of Nick when he opened the back hatch. He'd probably shoot her but being shot was better than being gutted on a cactus. Quicker, anyway.

The driver's side door opened, then slammed closed. The crunch of footsteps, and Nick's face appeared in the back window, a lighted headlamp centered on his forehead. His eyes flicked down to her bent legs. He smiled the coldest smile she'd ever seen and shook his head. His face disappeared from the window.

She held her position. She would not go meekly to the slaughter.

The hatch popped open, revealing only darkness. Then Nick lunged from the side, took hold of the shackles binding her legs, and jerked. She slid out and landed hard on the ground. Pain shot from her tailbone up her spine.

Nick yanked her to her feet by one arm and dug the muzzle of his pistol into her side. "Do what I tell you, and I'll shoot you in the head. Otherwise, you'll die like the others."

He dragged her away from the road toward a saguaro with an arm just a few feet off the ground. At the sight of it, her knees went weak. She stumbled into Nick and nearly knocked both of them over.

He staggered but regained his balance. His hand tightened around her bicep, and he shook her. "Knock that shit off."

He was right. She did need to knock that shit off if she wanted to survive. She scanned her surroundings and spotted a teddy bear cholla, its silver-white spines glowing in the light of Nick's head lamp. The ground beneath was littered with balls and young plants.

She rammed into Nick, and he toppled. She went down too, but she fell on him. He fell on the cholla.

He shrieked and tried to throw her off. She clung to his jacket with both hands and shifted her knees to drive his gun arm harder against the spines. With her hands and feet bound, she couldn't fight. Her only weapons were her weight and the cholla.

He twisted under her and slammed her arms against the cactus. She stifled a scream and jerked away.

Nick's arm rose, and the light from his head lamp glinted off the pistol barrel. She raised her arms in front of her—like they'd stop a bullet—and found her sleeves covered in cholla balls.

She threw her arms forward and rammed her cholla-studded elbows into Nick's face. He clawed at her, but she did it again, this time smashing a cholla ball into his eye. Then she scrabbled to her feet and stumbled toward the road.

She tripped on a rock and nearly fell. Without Nick's headlamp, she couldn't see more than shadows. She slowed and listened. Yelling and cursing. No footsteps.

Where was the road?

The sound of an approaching helicopter drowned Nick's howls, and the desert around her lit up like daylight. Police helicopters with searchlights. Vickie held her arms above her head, and the choppers slowed. One landed a few hundred feet from her, its blades spraying her with desert dust.

She didn't care. She sagged in relief and shuffled toward the chopper. Two officers emerged with guns drawn.

She stopped and raised her cuffed hands. "I'm Vickie Carmona, I'm—"

Her words were cut off by an arm clamped around her throat.

***

Carmona punched the answer button on his steering wheel, and Grimes' voice spoke over the car speakers. "They found her. She's alive."

"Thank the Lord." The sky in front of him was lit by a helicopter searchlight. "I'm almost there."

He ended the call, stomped the gas, and prayed he wouldn't pop a tire on the rocky road.

The helicopter held position, illuminating an area just ahead of him. Grimes hadn't mentioned a suspect in custody, so why wasn't the chopper pilot searching the area?

He rounded a turn and saw two figures illuminated in the searchlight beam. Vickie, upright and apparently unhurt. And a man behind her with an arm around her neck and a gun to her temple.

He slammed the brakes and cut the engine and headlights. The perp didn't react. Must not have heard the car over the chopper noise. Still, Carmona eased out of the vehicle as silently as he could and left the door open. He crept forward, eyes locked on the man, weapon drawn. He maneuvered behind the two figures, aimed, and fired.

***

Carmona bent over Vickie, who sat sidesaddle in the passenger seat of his car and busied himself pulling cholla spines out of her ankles with a pair of long nose pliers. Neither had looked the other in the eye since he'd shot Nick Harris dead.

A shoe scuffed behind him. He straightened and turned. Grimes said, "Bentley's here." She looked pretty grim for someone who'd just helped bust a serial killer.

"How'd you convince him to send the choppers?"

She looked grimmer. "I didn't. I went over his head to Chief

TROUBLE in Tucson

Flores. Told him about your wife," she cut her eyes to Vickie, then back to Carmona, "and that you were being framed and Bentley was falling for it. Probably fucked—sorry, messed up my career."

Carmona's lips twitched. "Grimes, you can curse in front of me all you like. And I'll make sure nothing," he hesitated, "screws up your career."

"Thanks, Detective."

She walked back to the scene. Bentley slammed his car door and stalked past Carmona as though he were a cactus. Carmona returned his attention to Vickie and the cholla spines.

When he'd pulled the last one, she broke the silence between them. "I suppose you know about Nick and me."

"Yeah. Well, I guessed. And I suppose you know about Dana."

"Nick told me."

"I'm sorry," they both said simultaneously.

"Jinx, you owe me a Coke." The words slid out before he could stop them, an old habit from their courtship that hadn't yet died.

Vickie looked up at him and gave him a shaky smile. "You got it."

~*~

133

THE BOYS WERE SEEN

PATRICK WHITEHURST

Terry Carson parked his red Ford Ranger in the Monterey Village parking lot, just under the sign's shadow. Not that it cast much of a shadow at one in the morning, just what the dusty streetlights created. He always swung into the same spot. Didn't feel right on the rare nights it was taken. Carson never had much cause to be there during the day. He knew it would be a different story then. Parking lot would be full of cars, full of people too, and he didn't like that.

Night air washed over him. A cool seventy-five under the moon. Never needed a blazer in the summer, only he always wore one over his Cuban Guayabera shirts. Tonight, he wore a black Haggar blazer, slim fit with two buttons, over a peach Guayabera. Gray slacks and black Oxford dress shoes finished the ensemble, except for the Heckler and Koch VP9 tactical pistol strapped under his shoulder. Kept the silencer on hand for quick access. Those two were the reason he wore the blazer.

A car sped east on Speedway as he made his way to the gated door between the bookstore and the massage place, both closed. He rapped his knuckles once on the frame. A second later he heard a series of locks come undone. Bernie greeted him from the other side.

He raised an eyebrow. "Carson! What's up?"

"Don't know yet."

"Knew you were coming, but Alan ain't said why." He stepped aside to let the taller man enter and locked it all up behind him. Bernie's generous gut made it tough to pass him in the brick-lined hallway. The place felt stuffy.

"Called me in so it can't be good," Carson said.

"How's that Ranger holding up? Those things, like the unofficial mascot of Tucson. They're everywhere." Bernie nodded to the end of the hall with a quiet burp. "He's waiting in his office. Just turned on Perry."

Carson went on alone, passing under bare yellow bulbs, and spotted Stephen and Vic at the end of the line. They flashed him a 'what's up' with their chins and continued chewing their toothpicks. Hallway turned right into the parlor. Past that he'd find Alan's office. Couldn't be too bad if he took the time to turn on Perry Mason. Man loved his courtroom drama. So did Carson.

The parlor looked like the inside of an Italian restaurant. Couple of dining room tables for the boys to play cards on, covered in red and white checks, some ferns gone brown, and two seventy-inch flat screens on the wall played the news and a recorded NBA game from earlier that night. Suns were about to make the finals again. Had all of Arizona perky. Three open pizza boxes from NYPD Pizza lay on one of the tables. He didn't see a single veggie on them.

Alan's office door was open, but he stopped before entering, knocked once on the wall. Might have been busy in there.

The old man's gravelly voice called out. "That you, Terry? Come on in."

Thick cigar smoke hung like a storm cloud in the center of the room. Man liked his Montecristos. Kept a mint of them on his mahogany desk in an ivory humidor. Red brick walls, adorned with portraits of the Tucson Crowd, one of the nicknames for members of The Family that lived in the Old Pueblo, closed around the smoke. A wood-framed Joseph Bonanno, done in heavy oils, hung over the desk, centered to be the first things visitors saw when they entered. Various other figures lined the side walls, all painted on canvas, including Alan Altavilla himself. He had more hair back when it was painted, black and luxurious. Another flatscreen blared on Carson's right as he walked into the center of the room.

"Terry, take a seat. Might need you on this thing," Alan said.

Altavilla was broad and stout, his gut like two side-by-side basketballs. He stood hunched over most of the time, but Carson rarely saw him out of that heavy-duty office chair. He wore his usual black cotton button-up and crimson red tie. White hair slicked back to show off his large forehead. No blazer. He waved his ham hock of a hand to a chair located in front of the desk. There were two, with one occupied. Claude sat in the chair to his right. The wispy-haired, scrawny meth head had his attention on the TV. Carson took a seat, keeping his eyes on the boss. One more body in that room and Carson would get restless.

"Situation's brewing," Alan said. "Remember that Miguel character trying to get a toehold on the Eastside?"

"Hey, Boss," Claude interrupted. "We got a twenty bet, remember?"

The old man looked confused for a second, and a bit dark at having been cut off, then showed off his dentures with a toothy grin. "What the hell," he said. "Got time. Terry, Claude here thinks you won't be able to name the episode. Thinks you need to see more than a few seconds. I bet twenty you'd nail it."

Carson turned to the flatscreen. Bethel Leslie, he remembered. The actor appeared on more than one episode of Perry Mason. In this scene, Raymond Burr spoke close to her, both dripping in black and white noir. Something about extortion.

"Time's up," Claude said.

"Case of the Wayward Wife," Carson said. "1959, episode eighty-two, I think."

Altavilla erupted in belly-shaking laughter. He held out his hand to Claude, who reluctantly slapped down a Jackson. "Told you my boy knew his Mason!"

Claude shook his head. "Just from a few seconds. Damn."

"Now turn that down so I can hear myself talk. Need anything, Terry? Hennessy? Coffee? Want me to send Bernie across the street for some Mexican from Molina's? May be closed, but they'll whip up something for me."

"Thanks, Alan. Coffee sounds good, with a splash of Henny." Carson figured the booze might help with his enochlophobia, at least keep the shakes down. Crowds weren't his thing.

"Heard the man, Claude. Bring in some of that pizza while you're out there."

Carson got back to business. "Don't remember any Miguel. Sure you told me about this?"

Alan shook his head. "Forget it. This Miguel kid made moves. Dealt in pills mostly, fentanyl, a girl or two. Wouldn't play nice. Had Bruce and Smashy take care of him. Knew you were taking a few weeks off after that last job."

"Only three days into those few weeks, Alan."

"Yeah, yeah. You think I don't know that? Miguel was an easy mark, and the boys wanted a turn, so they managed it. Snatched the kid down near Twenty-Second and Swan outside of a taco truck. Took him out to Vail for the hit, trail off Colossal Cave Road where they could dump him. Let him cool off a few days before some jogger finds him. You know the drill."

Carson nodded.

"Boys were seen. Like a pair of newbs those two. They'd just dragged the young man into a little gulch or whatever, threw sticks on him, and realized someone was out there with their ankle biter, little yapper dog. Pulled out the guns but didn't catch up in time. That's when I called you. Smart enough to have followed the witness to a home on Golden Oaks. They called as you were coming in. Got the house surrounded."

"Golden Oaks?" Carson's eye narrowed. "Probably already called the cops."

"Matter, Terry? Look pale," Alan said. "Witness went straight for a bottle in the kitchen. Smashy's sending updates. Out there would be County Sheriff's, I think. Case things go sideways, I'll want you on standby."

Claude ambled back into the smoke-filled office. He plopped a paper plate ladened with greasy pizza slices in front of the boss. Handed a white mug to Carson filled about two thirds with jet black coffee. Cream would have been nice, but he could smell the cognac, which made up for it. Alan stared at his cell phone, plopped his fat Montecristo in an ashtray, and whispered.

"Old lady from the looks of it. All of four and half feet with gray hair done up in a beehive. And get this, Terry." Alan turned his cell phone. Carson leaned forward, setting the coffee on the boss's massive desk. No coaster.

Smashy had sent over a video. Showed a woman in a blue terrycloth bathrobe downing a shot of brown liquid. The video panned right to a TV above a fireplace. Perry Mason on the screen, having words with Hamilton Burger. William Talman, one of the best. No mistaking that son of a bitch, even wobbly and shot through a window. Looked like "The Case of the Garrulous Go-Between." 1964. Episode seventy-two.

Smashy whispered into the phone from his hiding spot. "Funny, right? Guess we're all Mason fans here. Want us to go in, Boss?"

Carson shook his head as Alan set the phone down to reach for a slice. A hunk of pepperoni and mozzarella died between his lips.

He kept his voice steady. "Don't send them in, Alan."

Teeth smacked as he barked. Specks of red, greasy Italian shot out. "The Hell not? Hold on fellas." The last he said into the phone.

Carson felt Alan's eyes on him. He might have been sizing him up. Terry had come from back East. Been in Tucson a little over a year and had already proved his worth. Silenced a Fed on the last hit. Quick and easy. He and Alan had bonded over Raymond Burr.

"Terry, what's up? Looking squirrely over there."

"Bring the boys home, Alan," Carson said. Voice steady.

"Why?"

"Because that's my mom."

The slice fell from his hand. The air itself seemed to stop circulating oxygen. Altavilla's eyes narrowed. "Get out. That little old lady watching Perry Mason's your mother?"

"Bring them in, Alan."

"You never said your mother lived in Tucson. Why?"

Carson slid a hand under his blazer. "Not the sort of thing I talk about. We're not close, haven't spoken to her in years. Still wanted to watch over her."

Smashy breathed heavily on the other end of the video call. "Did I hear right. This Carson's ma?"

Alan held up his chubby palms in mock surrender. "Not in years? Terry, how we know she isn't gonna cry to the police?"

"We bail, right Boss?" Smashy interrupted. "We can't whack..."

"Stay put, boys." Alan's attention returned to Carson.

Carson's fingers felt the butt of the Heckler and Koch under the blazer. So much smoke in the room, no one could see what he was doing. Claude stood somewhere behind him. Probably had his eyes on the classic TV show. "You need to guarantee she won't mouth off, Terry. You can do that? You can look me in the eyes and tell me that?"

Glad he put the coffee down. Made things easier for what was to come. "No, I can't. Alan, you don't understand. My mom..."

Alan sighed. His eyes dropped regretfully to the cell. "Go in boys. Has to be done."

Smashy's voice shook. "Y-you sure, Boss? I mean...?"

"Go in, damn you!"

The line went dead. Alan ignored it and reached for his stogie. His pizza forgotten. Carson wondered what Claude was up to. The boss puffed on his Montecristo like a locomotive.

"Listen, Terry. Don't got a choice in this. Let's you and I have a drink. I know..."

Carson leaned forward. "Didn't let me finish. I'm not worried about my mom. But your boys, well, they're probably dead by now."

Alan's jaw dropped. Cigar nearly wiped out in his lap. It managed to hang on, glued by dried spit to his lower lip. "What? Terry, come on."

Claude chimed in over his shoulder. "What kind of crap you talking?"

Carson kept his eyes on the boss. "Who you think taught me, Alan? Bruce and Smashy have no idea what they're in for."

Alan already had the phone in his hands, stogie tucked back into the corner of his mouth, and started a return video call. Only no one answered. Could be they were still taking care of business. Could be they'd been taken care of.

Carson curled his index finger over the trigger. Kept it all under the blazer. "Mia Carson, otherwise known as Mia Giacomini, before she married my dad. Street called her Madame Bam. Stupid name, but I ate it up as a kid."

Beads of sweat marched down the old man's expansive forehead. Flesh had gone pale. "Maybe I'll have words with her. If she's Family, there's no way she'd go to the cops," Alan said. "Explains why she didn't call right away..."

"Went straight, Alan. I can't say for sure what she's going to do. She's been retired since 2004."

Cellphone chirped. Alan swiped it on, feeling relieved. "Bruce is calling, thank God." Only he didn't see Bruce's face. No bloody crime scene either. An old woman, her face too close to the camera, glared at him. Jet black eyes, strands of wrinkles on either side. Low roof above her, upholstery like a car. Call went dead again. Alan dropped the phone to the desk as if it burned his fingers. He flung the plate of pizza off the edge and cursed.

"Mom?" Carson asked.

"How'd she get Bruce's phone?"

Carson tensed. "Not hard for her."

Alan looked up at Claude, gave a slight nod. "Gonna have to track her down, Terry. Jesus, what are the odds?"

"Not me, Alan. Not doing it," Carson said.

"Gonna have to take a side. Don't talk to her anymore. Said so yourself." Smoke covered his face, puffing like a bellows.

Carson kept his mouth shut.

Claude's face materialized over his left shoulder once again. Close enough he smelled the alcohol in the meth-head's mouth. "I'll take it, Boss," he said. "Old lady can't be all that..."

Carson squeezed the trigger.

Claude fell back without a peep. Hit the floor just as the smoking VP9 tactical pistol emerged from Carson's ruined blazer. The blast rang in his ears. Nothing he could do about it. He popped off a shot at Alan, who wiggled too late to get out of his chair. The boss slumped down in a puff of rich, Cuban cigar smoke. The Montecristo fell from his lips.

Carson dropped to one knee and spun around. Fancy chair toppled on its side. He aimed the 9mm at the open door, footsteps charging his way. Stephen, Vic, and their gnawed toothpicks to the rescue. Only they never came in. Something had their attention. Faint pops at the front door. Bernie shouted incoherently. Two booms, louder now, with a thud as a body fell dead to the floor. Carson knew that sound. Unmistakable.

Vic's head appeared briefly at the entrance. Mouth formed an O, toothpick tumbled out, as he spotted Carson and pulled back. Carson kept his finger on the trigger. Didn't fire. Should that head appear again he knew just where to aim.

Then he saw it, a wisp of blue fabric passing through the haze of smoke. A flash of fire erupted, a zip of lightning across the room, and Stephen staggered into the office clutching his chest. Carson ignored him, spotted Vic again. As Stephen toppled over in the corner, Vic got off a shot at the blue blur that went wild. Hit the bricks on the far wall. The blue fabric vanished. He recognized the color. It matched the terrycloth robe he'd seen on the video call. Madame Bam in the house. He wasn't surprised she knew how to find the place.

Alan's gravelly voice, barely audible due to the ringing in Carson's ears, said, "Damn it, Terry. You're a good kid." Alan's hard fingers grabbed a fistful of hair and yanked Carson's head back. Alan kicked the gun from Carson's hand. A ham hock fist landed like a Boeing on his jaw.

Shots rang out from the parlor. Carson felt dizzy, surprised at the old man's strength. Blood filled his mouth. Altavilla had a hole in his chest, which glistened wetly over his black cotton button-up. The bullets must have missed his vitals. The man was a bull.

The boss pulled the younger man closer to him, mussing Carson's pricy Guayabera. "Some hitman. Didn't hear me coming." Fist pulled back for a second hit, followed by a loud pop from the doorway. Ham hock let go and fell away.

Carson blinked, wishing he'd paid more attention to his

surroundings. He'd missed the old man come up behind him, missed the shooter too. Altavilla lay unmoving at the foot of his desk, near a slice of uneaten pizza.

He turned and saw a .44 leveled at his head. She'd aged a bit since he'd seen her last. White beehive looked the same, except for the strands that came unraveled and hung over her dark eyes. She wore a white cotton sleep dress under the blue terrycloth robe. Fuzzy red slippers on her feet. Not a drop of blood on her. The gun wavered.

"See you're driving that Ranger into the ground."

He really had missed her. In so many ways. "Can't hear all that well at the moment," he replied.

Madame Bam glanced at the TV screen. Mason continued to play, he realized, despite the carnage. "Wayward Wife," she said. "Tragg was good in this one. God rest his soul."

~*~

ONE NIGHT AT FRED'S

ELENA SMITH

1991

"Please, let's not go to Fred's tonight," I begged as I climbed into the green Chevy monster truck. "It's Memorial Day weekend."

Before I could get the door closed, Mickie jammed on the accelerator and the beast vroomed away from the curb in front of my tan stucco apartment building. I launched back into the seat, holding the passenger door arm rest and swearing. The muffler-less engine chug-chug-chugged all the way down my street.

Mickie, a wiry blonde, and Martie, an athletic brunette, laughed. They would. Behind their backs they were called "The Wild Girls." These were ladies who didn't wear common western rowel spurs. They wore jingle bobs and carried buck knives on their leather belts. We'd been friends forever, riding the back trails and low Mountains near Tucson and competing against each other in barrel racing.

They knew my history with Wes and why I didn't want to go to Fred's Arena, even though it had the best hamburgers around. Saturday nights, Wes sat at the bar sucking down beers that left a sloppy remainder on the front of his shirt. The toned abs he'd sported in his bull-riding days were long gone. Now he was just a rodeo has-been who liked to hear himself talk while country music played in the background. This included an endless supply of hero stories from his days in Viet Nam and the wild goings-on during the Summer of Love. His best friend Wally, a cop, would sit next to him and laugh at his recycled jokes.

Round-faced Martie flipped her brunette hair and lightly hit my cheek with the perfumed ends.

"Oh, Crystal, I know you don't love Wes anymore," she said in her throaty alto, "but I kind of dig him. Maybe I should go for him."

"Be my guest, if you're that desperate."

"You never said he was bad in bed," Mickie countered, long blonde hair framing a chiseled face. "Is he?"

I crossed my arms over my bust.

"Oh, she's not tellin'," Martie laughed. "I don't know if that's a good sign or a bad one."

I harumphed a sigh. I never admitted my true feelings for Wes to anyone, not even my best friends. They wouldn't understand.

"You'll find someone new," said Martie. "There'll be plenty of guys there tonight. One of 'ems gotta be cute and not broke."

Thankfully, when we pulled into the gigantic dirt parking lot in front of Fred's Arena, miles from the edge of town, there was no sign of the 1989 maroon-colored Ford F250 usually covered in dust and hitched up to an aluminum stock trailer. Wes was not here. At least not yet.

When we got inside, Martie turned out to be right as she usually was. Even though the three of us were pushing thirty, we weren't too old for the singles scene. There was plenty of eye candy for every age range.

We walked toward a round eight-seater table in the center of the room and a cute guy caught my eye as we passed him. He was slim with long brown hair and a moustache, and a blue and white striped roping shirt.

"Hey, doll," he said, reaching out his hand and grasping my forearm.

Sometimes I liked that approach, sometimes I didn't. I stopped in my tracks to look him in the eyes. They were hazel eyes, large and soulful. Looked fairly harmless. I wasn't sure about the age gap, though. He was about twenty-one to my twenty-nine. But for

146

just one night, who cared about that?

Mickie and Martie pulled up short behind me and I heard a lascivious chuckle that signaled approval.

"Why don't you three beauties sit down here and join me? I'll buy the first round."

So, we did. The odds were off, three gals to one dude, but that would change when the place filled up. This young guy was obviously attracted to me. I knew why. A lot of cowgirls were so skinny they looked like boys. I had an hourglass figure and men picked me out a crowd like a horse found every flower bud buried in its alfalfa.

I agreed to let this guy start buying us beers because I already knew I could hand him off to one of my friends as the evening wore on. Still, it was a stupid way to start the night. I knew what would happen and the Wild Girls did, too. At some point, Wes would walk into Fred's and come to our table and invite himself to join us. Little by little, he'd out-talk and overpower any other males around and I was so weak I'd let it happen. I always did.

There was no good reason why I still loved him. I'd seen him at a rodeo just after I'd turned eighteen. I didn't care that he was twenty-eight. We'd never lived together, although he proposed several times after he left his young family and finalized the divorce. Now, he was fat and overbearing, but he had been the first love in my life, and I hadn't been able to shake him. Wes was the kind of guy that, if you gave him any encouragement, he owned you. His claws never loosened. And, here I was at Fred's Arena on a Saturday night ready to let him take me home as he had so many times in the past.

Our new friend told us his name was Booker. He and his horse had recently moved here from Tempe. Booker was excited to be twenty-one and his lack of conversational skills showed it. He rattled off a list of his favorite brands of beer, bragged about his truck, and told us he liked to listen to rap music. Mickie and Martie tried to help him with his goal to impress me, but it was useless. My eyes wandered to Fred's front door as I watched for Wes's arrival.

I turned my attention back to Booker, who was doing a coin

trick with his hands. His fingers were long and slender, like those of a good guitar or piano player. I looked up and saw the way he watched me, wanting to know if he'd caught my interest yet. Then, I realized what I found attractive about him. He had hazel eyes, like Wes did. It always came back to Wes.

Around ten o'clock, the front door opened across the room and first Wally entered, short and thin with nerdy black-framed glasses and a bald spot in the middle of his brown hair. Behind him was Wes, stuffed into a brown plaid shirt that stretched so tight over his gut the buttons were ready to pop. I sighed as I waited for my heartbeat to ease. Love is something that can't be explained by anyone besides the one who feels it.

The two men worked their way through the room crammed full of drinkers who laughed, hooted and hollered as the work week's stress disintegrated into the festive weekend atmosphere. They headed for our table, like a cattle dog that knows which calf to cut from the herd.

I snuck a look at the girls. They were ogling Booker hopefully. His eyes were still on me. I met his gaze.

"So, if ya'd like to go out for a trail ride some moonlit night..." he was saying.

I felt myself nodding while my mind said, 'I don't think so.' If I didn't take him home with me tonight, nothing would happen. And now that Wes and Wally had come along, well, nothing was going to happen. He was a cute guy; he'd find someone to ride into the sunset with even if it was temporary.

Booker gazed into my eyes with romantic intent. "I'm free tomorrow night."

Tossing her blonde hair, Mickie said, "Or tonight. There's a full moon this evening."

A strong thigh hit the back of my metal-framed chair sending a spiderweb of pain through my spine just like it had the day I'd made a bad landing after an untrained horse bucked me off. I didn't turn and look. I knew who it was and what he wanted. A strong paw put pressure on my left shoulder. More spinal pain from a previous injury.

"Hey, Honey Bunny Bun-Bun," Wes's baritone boomed above my head.

My eyes shot to Booker who had an odd look on his face. Anger. Rage. An over-reaction to Wes's comment? Was he feeling jealous or was it about his ego? Was he the kind of guy who got hot when he drank? I was about to find out. He shot out of his chair.

"What did you say?" he challenged, the knuckles of his fists on the tabletop.

Wes rested both hands on my shoulders. "What's it to you, stranger?"

Booker's eyes became slits.

"Honey Bunny Bun-Bun," Martie jeered.

"That's his special name for her," Mickie said as if she thought an explanation was helpful.

Wes, never the type to miss a potential fight, moved away from me and around the table toward Booker. "You have a problem with that?"

He moved toward Booker in a slow measured walk, but he didn't see what he was walking up to. Booker had a knife on his belt and it was in his right hand and sunk deep into Wes's chest before the older man saw it coming. Wes's eyes bulged in surprise as Booker glared at him.

We all jumped to our feet, disbelieving what our eyes told us. A large red stain spread across the front of Wes's shirt. He sank to his knees. Even Wally, an experienced deputy, froze with shock. Booker, whose youthful confidence knew no bounds, bent over and withdrew his knife. Wes's hands groped the leaking empty spot on his shirt pocket.

The Wild Girls screamed for help.

Wally took charge.

"Is there a medic in the house?"

He whirled on Martie. "Damn it, girl, you're a medical assistant; get down on the floor and help him. Stanch the flow!"

She did as he said, pulling a bandana out of her back pocket to push against the wound.

Booker's expression was calm, as if he'd set this all up and done it on purpose which, of course, he couldn't have done.

Wally moved with surprising speed for a man pushing fifty. He grabbed Booker's right wrist forcing him to drop the knife on the floor. With his other hand he grasped a pair of handcuffs from the back of his waist, snicked them open and before Booker knew what hit him he was in full detention. Wally then kicked him hard in the ankles and he buckled to the floor.

It all happened so fast we could hardly describe it later when we gave our statements. One minute we'd been drinking and joking around. Then, Wes had made some remark and Booker went ballistic. Now, Martie and I did the best we could to keep Wes comfortable until the ambulance came. Wally had Booker sitting up, ankles tied together and hands cuffed behind his back.

The EMTs arrived quickly and carried Wes away. Wally was stuck watching Booker until someone could deliver a squad car.

Through choking sobs, I said, "How could you do it, Booker? What could possibly have made you so mad?"

Booker began rambling. "Mama said he was dead. She said he was killed in 'Nam. I never thought — " He choked back a sob. "I never thought I'd kill him, but I had to."

I snuck a look at Wally who suppressed a smirk that seemed inappropriate for the circumstances.

"What did your mama have to do with any of this?" I continued.

"Mama told me he was dead, that he died in 'Nam right before I was born. She told me I had a hero for a dad because he gave his life for our country. If he hadn't been killed, he was gonna come home and marry her and we'd be a family. But that's not how it went. He didn't die. He didn't come back. And he never contacted either of us."

He looked into my eyes, to be sure I could see his pain. But that wasn't what I saw. I saw a pair of hazel eyes that looked like Wes's and I knew what he was saying. Wes was his biological father, a father he hated because he'd been abandoned before birth. But how did he know to find Wes at Fred's Arena in Tucson, because they were both from Tempe? Was it just a coincidence they were there tonight? Did their mutual DNA draw them to this place and this ending?

Mickie and Martie had watched the whole thing unfold without saying a word. That was a first for The Wild Girls. Finally, Mickie spoke.

"How did you know he was your real dad?"

Booker lowered his eyes in sorrow. "It was what she always said. She told me he called her 'Honey Bunny Bun-Bun.' It was his special name for her."

He looked daggers at me as if I'd stolen the nickname from his mother, and I shivered.

The front door of Fred's opened. A troop of cops walked in to take Booker to jail. One of them read him his Miranda rights and they marched him out the door with Wally following close behind, heading toward his truck. I scampered after the balding deputy.

"Wally — ?"

He turned to face me. "What, Crystal? We'll be in touch with you for your statement. I have to go to the station to file a report."

"Is he going to be okay?"

He looked away, his eyes following the squad car that carried Booker to jail, then looked back. "I don't know, hon. I hope so."

"But if he doesn't —?"

"You did a good job, Crystal."

"What do you mean?"

"You got him to say his motivation. It will make the case against him stronger."

"But he didn't get his Miranda before he said it — "

"Oh, that only counts if he was talking to me when he confessed. He wasn't talking to me he was talking to you. I was just a witness."

He winked at me as he let it all sink in. Now I understood why he smirked when Booker started babbling. The kid was making a case against himself, and Wally knew it.

Relief flooded me as he turned away and sprinted toward his pick-up truck. Ninety-degree heat radiated from the packed earth under my feet. A gazillion stars sparkled above me in the black sky. I put my face in my hands and bawled. Pretty soon, Mickie and Martie came up behind me. They wrapped their arms around me and held me close.

~*~

THE DOGS ARE BACK

EMMA PEREZ

"The dogs are back."

Obdulia hovers over the kitchen sink and scrubs gristle from a burnt pan. Through the window, she sees a blue sky dappled with saguaros pointing up like sentinels guarding the horizon. A pack of scraggly mutts scamper and toss an object in the air, chasing after it.

"They're playing with something. Looks dead," she says.

"Could be a mouse," says Fred.

Federica goes by Fred. She sits at the breakfast table, sips black coffee and rubs polish on a six-inch blade, spitting on willful spots.

"Smaller than that," says Obdulia.

"A lizard then."

Obdulia shakes her head once and stares out the window trellis in a trance.

Fred shoves the knife in a leather belt holster, stands, and pulls open the back door. She skips down three concrete steps and greets the dogs running to her, bouncing and darting. Fred rubs the black stocky one under its chin. The reddish-brown dog flaps its ears eagerly, nudging for a turn. The other three mutts are still flinging the item and the petite chihuahua-whippet catches it with open jaws and chews.

"Give me that," says Fred.

She bends to pick up the thing and sees a finger, bruised yellow and bumpy. With her shirttail, she cradles the withered extremity and returns to the kitchen, dumping it on the marble counter. Obdulia joins her and they gape for a long minute.

"I'll call Remy," says Fred.

"Of course, you will."

"Seriously, Duli?"

Obdulia shrugs her shoulders and examines the dried digit on her kitchen counter. She pokes it with a fork, turning the piece over.

"Look at this," she says. "A tattoo. Faded, but still. Could be a tattoo. Your Remy will love this."

"Let me see." Fred bends down to inspect it closely. It's probably a cut. Or the dogs' bite marks."

"Look closer." Obdulia sighs loudly and paces back, pushing Fred's head down. "This here."

"Stop it." Fred rubs the back of her head.

"Do you see it now?"

"See what? I don't know what I'm looking for."

"Por favor, Federica. Mira!"

Obdulia grazes the yellowed brown flesh with a fork, aiming at the faded design.

"Oh. Wow. Okay. Looks like infinity."

"Or an eight."

"Yeah. Or an eight." Fred pauses. "I'll go call Remy."

"Remy's an amateur."

Obdulia lifts a chili-stained apron over her head and hangs it on a doorknob. From the closet, she snatches a wide-brimmed straw hat and a waxed canvas backpack that she stuffs with an apple and almonds. A stainless-steel water bottle is filled to the brim, and she crams it into the side mesh pocket.

"Grab your hat," says Obdulia.

"Not after last time."

"Last time?"

"The police weren't happy."

"Fuck them. And ICE."

"At least let me call Remy."

"Fine. Call Remy."

Obdulia opens the kitchen junk drawer and pulls out a sandwich bag, hands it to Fred, who rolls the shriveled digit into the plastic and tosses it back on the counter.

"Put it in the fridge," says Obdulia.

"Not with my food I won't."

"Fine."

Obdulia rushes from the kitchen into morning heat. It's barely 9:00 A.M. and the sun already blisters the skin. Cicadas hum in unison. A white-striped mourning dove nests in the eaves by the back door and eyes Obdulia when she lingers to stare. The cooing soothes her most mornings, but not today. Already, she anticipates the horror of whatever might be in a desert that leads brown folks through corridors ensuring nothing but more hell. She follows the pathway through the shrubs of ragweed and cholla and admires ocotillo sprouting green buds. The elongated branches resemble a long-haired Medusa scaling the sky. Maybe an omen of hope. Maybe the finger got bitten off and the owner survived. Maybe there's not another death in the desert today. She hears Fred traipsing behind her.

"Hold up, Duli."

Obdulia stops and turns to look at Federica.

"Well?" says Obdulia.

"Well what?"

"Remy?"

"She says to leave it. They're sending a task force."

"Tucson's finest? When?"

"She's not sure. By the end of the week."

"Great."

Obdulia strides faster through prickly shrubs. Her long beige pants protect her from the pokes and stabs of barrel cacti and furry teddy-bear cholla.

"Wait! Would you please wait?"

"Well fucking hurry up, Fred. Not like I'm stopping you."

Obdulia relaxes her speed and Fred catches up. They struggle through bushes as Fred drives her oak walking stick, probing and launching a footpath.

"I don't know why you get so pissed at me," says Fred.

"I don't know what you mean."

"Yeah, right."

Obdulia shoves her body in front of Fred and breathes into the crevice of her neck, glaring, attempting to put Fred on alert but Fred glares back and breathes warm air on her face. They crack smiles.

"You think you're so damn tough, Duli."

"Here's a surprise, you know I'm so damn tough. That's why you're with me and not that fashion cop."

"Fashion cop?"

"You've never heard that before?"

"Nope."

"I made it up."

"And what the fuck is it supposed to mean?"

"Oh, please. Isn't it obvious?"

"She's a good cop, Duli."

"So say you."

They continue hiking through desert cholla that sheds clusters of brown spikes on the beige folds of their pants. They both wear khakis and while Fred's have a vertical line ironed down the middle of each leg, Obdulia's are wrinkled and soiled with bacon grease and buttered toast.

Obdulia breaks and points toward something in the distance; when she studies the thing, she realizes the mirage is nothing more than a Saguaro with a budding head like a child's pressing against the back of a woman or man trekking through the wilds. It's deceiving. She looks intently at the towering plant because it appears stately and mobile like a parent hiking with their child strapped securely on their back, fully fed, and curiously observing plants and bugs. But it's only a mirage. She has to check herself, keep from imagining things she wants to see. Brown people crossing borders from south to north are not hiking leisurely. They run from bloody carnage escaping lies and history. They want a miracle. We all do, she thinks.

Fred passes her and stands on an incline. She waves at Obdulia to join.

"Down there," says Fred.

"What is it?"

"Not sure. Another body part?"

"Damn. Well, let's go see."

"We can't disturb the crime scene."

"Ay Federica. Siempre lo mismo."

"Leave it. For now, Duli. Please."

"Fuck you, Fred. I'm gonna go see."

Obdulia slides downhill over clumps of dirt, freeing rocks and pebbles. She skids, showering dust on her shoes and pants; as she lands at the bottom, she stumbles, trying to avoid landing on a fleshy mass. Regains her balance. Jornada de Muerte, she thinks. She'd seen the signposts on her drive from Tucson to Albuquerque. Not far from here, but close enough. Mostly through New Mexico and the flats of the Texas Panhandle. The Journey of Death is mottled with buried skeletons of settlers who trekked from east to west, unaware or just plain stupid. Only local tribes and their merged families navigate the terrain with ease. Thing is, the route doesn't reach south into the Sonoran Desert. Still, Obdulia imagines the brown people who risk a death journey for something else. Hope, she guesses. Some brand of hope must make the trip worthwhile or maybe they aren't hopeful at all, fully aware they'll probably dry up in the hot sun. Each in-drawn breath feeling like suffocation.

She stands over the dead rabbit. It's squishy with a round little belly. Could have died of heat exhaustion or maybe it fell from above, hiding from a predator and hit its tiny head on a boulder. Hard to say.

"Anything?" Fred yells.

Obdulia digs a small grave with a sharp rock, pushes the rabbit inside with the toe of her shoe and shoves sandy dirt on the creature. She picks up two twigs, threading a thin shred of bark around the middle of the crossed limbs, ties them and plants the make-shift cross on top of the grave.

Fred watches from above and waits for a response.

157

"Hey, should I join you?"

Obdulia looks up, her hand a brim shading her eyes, then ambles down a path farther into sweltering air. She gazes at the sky and sees the sun overhead. Must be noon, she thinks.

"There's nothing out here, Duli."

But she continues moving away from the voice.

"Time to turn back. Come on. You'll get heat-stroke."

Fred wouldn't let her forget the time she ventured into the scorching landscape, forging ahead as she was prone to do. They'd been hiking at Organ Pipe National Monument and out of nowhere, she tripped on skeletal remains. At first, she thought she had discovered an animal, a deer or javelina. All she saw were loose bones, dazzling white under golden sun. The blinding white arched shapes caught her attention. A rib? A hip bone? With her walking stick, she flipped the pieces aside and noticed a buried tip of a rounded ball the size of a melon. Quickly, she dug out a skull, small and smooth. A cracked line could be traced across the left side to the temple. She had not forgotten how she felt, what she thought, the way she fainted. Remy had been with them and took over the "crime scene," rebuking Obdulia for having disturbed the remains. As if it mattered. As if anyone cared.

That they had discovered fragments of a young woman had angered Obdulia and the anger steeped inside her, not letting her rest. It was too much to be so close to the bones and spirit of someone now lost to their lover or child or parent. And it didn't help that Remy lectured her with statistics about desert deaths.

"In Pima County alone, there have been more than four hundred women over the last four decades who've died of heat exposure, or some undetermined way. Blunt force injury, too." Remy pointed to the crack on the skull. "About half of those, some two hundred or more, just skeletal remains. Unidentified. Sad, really."

Remy flitted above the bones that Obdulia had found and spoke so assuredly, so authoritatively that she wanted to sock the model cop in the face. Instead, she fainted.

She glances up to see Federica waving and shouting something incomprehensible, which only makes Obdulia want to hazard farther into the heat. She wants to ignore Fred, but decides to turn back; climbs up the hill, her cheeks red, temper seething.

"You look parched," says Fred.

"I am parched."

Fred places a water bottle at Obdulia's lips. She sips slowly, removes her hat and wipes her forehead with the back of her hand.

"Let's go back," says Fred.

Obdulia marches ahead, picking up the pace, once again leaving Fred behind. She needs to be alone. Without Fred's constant grilling.

"What do you want for dinner?" asks Fred.

"It's too early for dinner."

"I know. Just thought I'd make a run to the market."

"Fine."

"Look, we'll come back out tomorrow. I mean if you want."

"No point. Maybe your Remy will find something. That is, if her task force ever shows up."

"What have you got against her anyway?"

"Nothing. Not a thing."

Obdulia sprints now, eager to get home, longing to avoid more conversation. She's not sure why she's so enraged. She's not sure why Federica has such a calm demeanor. She doesn't know what to do anymore, how to do it, whatever it is she should be doing. It's as if the world is turned relentlessly upside down, so far from human kindness that all she can do is fume from the fucked-up world around her. She senses Federica near her.

"It's going to be okay, Duli. I promise."

"Would you do me a favor?"

"Of course. Anything. I'll do anything you want."

"Then, please, please shut the fuck up, Fred."

Fred drops back and when they arrive in their back yard, she picks up a red ball and tosses it in the air. The dogs scamper and fight for the toy.

Obdulia opens the back door and screams, not loud, but a scream more like a grunt announcing, 'I'm so tired.' She crouches on the floor, holding a plastic bag, shredded and empty.

~*~

SOMETHING EXTRA

KATHY McINTOSH

Madrone Hunter slowed as she drove past her favorite mural in Tucson—a wall of brilliant color, with a javelina and a jackrabbit riding bikes taking starring roles. She smiled. It was worth the slight detour on her way from her mother's home to meet her cousin.

She soon arrived at a home with a clean, fresh, just-painted appearance. Diego's pickup was in the driveway. Magnetic signs on the truck's side doors read Best Compadres Painting.

Why did her cousins need her help? What ridiculous promise had her mother made? She tried to shrug off her concern and avoid wishing she were home, catching up on all the things she'd left undone while out of town with Adventure Calls Ecotouring.

She got out of her much smaller pickup and smiled at her cousin. "Looks great, as usual," she said, waving her arms toward the home. "No big drips on the driveway or the sidewalk." She flashed him an evil grin and added, "Except you."

When her mother told her Diego and Tito needed her help, Madrone's first reaction was terror. When the brothers started their painting business, Madrone had hired on as an assistant. Because of her penchant for getting more paint on herself than on the house, she didn't last long. Her cousins had never let her forget her short career or her shortfalls at house painting.

When she'd phoned him to discuss why he needed her help, she said, "Please, please don't ask me to help you and Tito paint."

Diego burst into laughter so raucous she had to hold the phone away from her ear. "No way, Cuz. I have enough problems without you painting," he managed to gasp. After he'd recovered from his laughing jag, he said, "Tia Juanita told us how you solved two murders in your new job. Pretty cool. We need that brilliant detective brain of yours."

"Tia Juanita"—also known as Madrone's mother—"has an inflated idea of my detecting skills. I'm a cook, not a cop. I helped a friend find the first killer, and finding the second one was mostly a mistake."

"Not what your mother said. She also said you weren't working for Adventure Calls this week and that family always helps family."

Did Mom tell him how close I she came to being killed? Surely this isn't another murder for me to solve. Because I'm not sure I could go through that again. "If you promise no paint sprayers and no dead bodies, I'm yours for the rest of the week."

"Deal," he said and instructed her where to meet him. "It's easier to show you than describe."

Diego didn't laugh at her joke about him being the only drip on the driveway and his smile of greeting was tight, his hug cut short. Something bad had to have upset her normally laid-back relative.

Not tall, but muscular and fit, with dark hair cut close to his scalp, a carefully groomed mustache and intelligent brown eyes set beneath deep brows and enviable lashes, Diego easily drew women and men to him. Acne pockmarks on his face marred almost perfection and, along with that carefree smile, dissolved jealousy. She recalled the many times her cousin's easy-going approach to life had defused potential explosions in their family get-togethers. "Come on." He led her around to the front entrance of the home. Stopped, pointed at the wall.

About two feet up on a wide expanse of freshly painted stucco someone had used orange paint to create a graffiti tag about two feet high, three of those familiar balloon letters, with a snake's head at the top of the central G. DGT.

Recognition dawned. "Tell me it isn't—"

"It is. Our tag from our foolish youth."

Her cousins had misspent some of their teenage years as taggers, surreptitiously creating graffiti on bare surfaces throughout Tucson. Fortunately for them, they'd managed to evade arrest.

"You can come up with a better logo," she said. "One the cops won't recognize."

"Thanks for the advice, Cuz. And your mama called you brilliant."

He pulled a toothpick from his back pocket and Madrone wondered how he sat with those little spears so close to his butt. He popped it in one side of his mouth and chewed. "We finished the paint job here about two weeks ago. When we left, this place was pristine. Our usual excellent prep, painting, and cleanup." His words could have been a commercial for his service.

"A few days later, the owner phoned me. Not happy. Told me to get my… truck out here, fast. When he showed it to me, he said if it was my idea of a joke, it wasn't a good one. Told me to get rid of it before he sued." He cleared his throat. "I assumed some tagger had been here. We covered it with stain-blocking primer and repainted that section. Didn't think much of it until another client phoned me at home that night." He pulled out his phone and showed me photos of several different views of the same tag, in various colors, on different homes. "This client let me leave it here to show the cops—and now you. The cops aren't hopeful. Told me taggers are quick and stealthy, like I didn't know that. But jeez, they've hit five of our most recent jobs. I called other painters I know and none of them are having this problem. Or at least none of them will admit it."

"Weird, I agree. Any of your employees a possibility?"

"Think I didn't consider that already?" Diego shook his head. "Not a current employee. Probably no one who used to work with us, but the list's pretty long."

"And no one with a personal grudge against you…or Tito?"

"Not that we can think of." He scuffed his boot on the gravel around the elegant home. Every time we have to return to a site, it's money, and time lost."

Ah, money. That's what's often at the root of many crimes, Madrone speculated. Money and greed, or passions like jealousy or revenge.

Diego was happily married, as far as Madrone knew. If there'd been rumors about the state of his marriage, she'd have heard from her mother. All she heard from that source was news of Diego's adorable toddler and brand-new baby, and "when will I be a grandmother, mija?"

Diego's younger brother and partner Tito, however, was in his late twenties, single and dated a lot of women. One little mistake, dating someone casually who took you seriously, might have created a problem.

"Friends? Former friends? Maybe an ex who didn't like becoming an ex?"

"Are you accusing me of cheating on Diana? First, I'd never do that to her or my kids, and second, I wouldn't be alive to worry about my business if I did."

She shook her head. "I was thinking about Tito. He's cute and some woman might think he'd make a good catch."

He laughed at that one. "As if anyone could catch him. Tito makes it a point to date what he calls, 'confident women with lives of their own.' Maybe you don't remember the fiasco with Emma, that girl with the blue hair in high school?"

Madrone searched her memory banks but came up blank. "Nope."

"Thought she was someone from West Side Story, I guess, since she was in a rival tagging group. She used to come by our house, all times of the day and night. Got so Mama knew her better than Tito. Finally, Mama and a counselor from the school set her straight. Almost came to a restraining order." He chuckled. "But the girl made great empanadas. I gained weight from that episode. Since then, Tito's made it clear to the women he dates that he's not a serious investment." He took a deep breath and shook, like a dog after a swim. "C'mon, you gotta see the back of this house. I think a snob would call it irony." The last word spoken like a bad English professor.

164

She trailed him down an elaborate gravel pathway to the backyard. "So maybe an angry ex-boyfriend of one of those women?"

"Tito and I have gone there and come up blank." He stopped and swept an arm out. "Mira!"

The large backyard was landscaped, Tucson-style, with rocks, cactus, pavers, a swimming pool, and an outdoor kitchen that clutched at Madrone's heart. The now-standard for "elegant outdoor living" grill under a ramada of mixed iron and copper, an horno, or outdoor oven, a built-in wine fridge. She stifled her envy and let her gaze continue around the yard.

Her focus moved to the custom steel and iron furniture. Then a loud, long wolf whistle behind her made her jump, stumble and crash into Diego's back.

Large hands grabbed her shoulders and spun her into an embrace. "Surprise! It's your favorite cousin."

"You'll be my late cousin if you scare me like that again." Madrone fanned herself and worked to hide her grin.

Taller and thinner than his older brother, yet just as muscular, Tito considered himself a girl-magnet and often was. Diego might be wrong about an angry ex of Tito's working her revenge with that tag. But how could Madrone possibly find out, when there were so many exes in Tito's life?

"So," Tito asked, "what do you think?" He waved toward the back of the prestigious home. Beside floor-to-ceiling plate glass windows was a mural—part stained glass and part acrylic paint, a mesmerizing, bold-colored scene of ocean and desert. It reminded Madrone of Puerto Peñasco, better known as Rocky Point, a popular resort community just over 200 miles south of Tucson in the state of Sonora, Mexico.

"Ooh. I'm in awe. Who did it?"

"We hired someone to do the stained-glass tiles, and Tito and I did the painting." Diego beamed at her.

Of course. Her cousins had misspent some of their teenage years as taggers but were rescued from arrest by some older former taggers who were making money painting commissioned murals and hired the brothers as assistants. The brothers later started their house painting company after attending Pima Community College. And now, more than ten years later, they'd come full circle with this commission.

"Good job, you two. It's incredible."

His smile faded. "Yeah, except the owners threw a fit when they saw that little tag out front. Now I'm worried they won't recommend us to their friends. And we were just getting a wedge into this community. Bigger houses, better pay than mid-town and west. And more chance for stuff like this."

"Oh, no." Not fair, and it reeked of sabotage, from someone who had it in for her cousins and their company. But who, and why?

"You said it, 'oh, no.' We invested in some new equipment so we could take on these higher paying jobs. If they don't pan out—well." Diego shrugged. Tito shook his head.

"We can do this," Madrone said. "I'm not sure where to start, but I'd like a list of your former employees, and, if you have it, people who've applied to work for you. Also, who your biggest competitors are."

Diego frowned. "There's plenty of work in Tucson, so I can't see why a competitor would care. In fact, we belong to a group of small business owners that meets to discuss ways to build business without losing control."

Madrone smiled, possibly too much like a cat who'd caught a bird mid-flight. "I bet it's one of those groups who only let one of every kind of business in. When did you join, and who invited you?" She imagined someone blocked from such a group seeking revenge and ultimate replacement of her cousins in the group.

"When we first started Best Compadres Painting, eight years or so ago, we joined a group that was forming. Been there ever since."

"I'm just sayin'. . . people can hold a grudge for a long time."

"Maybe. Tito and I printed out both those lists for ourselves. I'll get them to you when we leave. But you're barking up the wrong tree."

"As long as I don't bite it, let me make that decision," Madrone said.

They meandered to the front of the home, Madrone wondering about the interior, given the elegance of the backyard. After her cousin gave her the printed sheets, she asked Tito for his take on the situation.

He flashed a grin. "I know you won't believe me, but it's not any of my exes. And anyone we let go understood why and couldn't hold a grudge." At her skeptical look, he added, "Really. If you get caught smoking weed on the job, you kinda know what's gonna happen. Same if you discover you're afraid of heights. Or can't make our early hours. There's always another job, just not with such excellent bosses." He spread his arms. "But we're counting on your detective powers. You're the one who caught a couple of murderers."

"More like stumbled on." She scanned the list. "If I'm gonna figure this out, I need help. If you don't think it's someone on these lists, I'd be wasting time checking each name out. And besides, I'm not the police or even a real private detective. I don't know how to do that." She tapped her lips with the sheets of paper. "When you were young, back in your wild days of tagging, did you tell the cops about any of your friends who also tagged? To get out of being arrested, maybe?"

Tito gave her a chilling look. "You're asking if we ratted out a friend? We didn't. It wasn't done. Honor among thieves and all that."

"How noble." She thought for a while. "We need to catch someone in the act."

"A stakeout," Tito cried. "Perfect!"

They decided to have her join Diego and Tito at their next job site in two days, only a few blocks from where they were. "One of us will talk to the owner, let him know we'll be hanging around after we normally stop painting."

"Not we. Just me. I'll take a camera. I doubt this person is dangerous, except to your bottom line."

Diego and Tito shared a look she couldn't decipher. "You're the boss on this one," Diego finally said.

Madrone arrived at Best Compadres' next painting site at 6:30 a.m. on the designated date, weighed down by a backpack filled with food and water for the stakeout, a good camera, a blanket, the solar charger for her phone—something she often made use of on tours—and doubts about the wisdom of this attempt to find the graffiti culprit. She wore painting overall shorts with a long-sleeved T-shirt, since she and her cousins had concluded that having her there as temporary help would allay the fears of a lurking vandal.

Other than discovering nothing to help her cousins, what she feared most was another humiliation in her painting career. She doubted she could outdo the time she tripped over a five-gallon container Diego was using to fill his sprayer. Who knew paint could splash that far? Or the first time he'd let her spray paint and she'd pointed the nozzle backward, something he told her was next to impossible to accomplish.

Knowing her history, Diego told the customer Madrone would be taking photos for their website instead of painting. "Actually, not a bad idea, Madrone," Tito said. "Show me what you end up with. Although if I'd known, I'd have spent more time with my grooming this morning." He swept a hand back over his hair, a useless gesture since it was tied back in the usual ponytail he wore for work.

After helping the brothers unload their equipment from the truck and move patio furniture and potted plants away from the home, she took out her camera equipment and went into undercover mode.

Watching the two painters, Madrone marveled at how smoothly and effectively they worked together, as if choreographed. No wasted motion, very little conversation except when the homeowner emerged with a question. No radio blaring, just quiet efficiency. No wonder they'd been receiving 5-star recommendations. She had to find out who was vandalizing their work and fast, before word got out and destroyed their business.

Tito paused his power-washing to saunter in front of her, his hair now loose and flowing, looking great in paint-spotted, baggy jeans. He smiled and posed. He grabbed the power washer. "Can you get this in a shot with me?" he said.

She could, if she backed up a bit. She focused on Tito and his equipment—the power washer, of course—and backed up a few steps more.

"Stop!" Tito yelled. "Madrone, watch out."

She stepped backward. Into the pool. "Cheese and rice!" She had fallen into the shallow end and held the camera above her head with one arm, flailing with the other. She waddled to the steps. She scowled at her cousin. "Help me out of here, bufón. Take the camera. Why didn't you warn me? This camera didn't come cheap."

Tito staggered toward her, laughing so hard he was powerless to help her. Eventually he reached out a hand and took the camera.

Diego walked around the side of the house and asked, "What is all the noise about?" Then he saw Madrone in the pool. He snickered. "Hey, Cuz, we didn't ask you here so you could go swimming. You'd think all that martial arts stuff in school would have made you more graceful."

Madrone scowled at him and dripped. "No comment." Tito had always been a prankster, but this went way too far.

The homeowner came out the back door and offered Madrone a change of clothes. "Come on inside. I'll put your clothes in the dryer." It was obvious to her that he was trying to stifle laughter. Belatedly, he asked if she was okay and she nodded and trailed after him into the home.

If she couldn't keep herself from falling into a pool, how was she going to find a tagger and stop the vandalism?

Madrone spent the rest of the afternoon alternately lounging on the patio and doing minor, easy tasks assigned to her by Diego. Tito was too busy making fun of her to ask her to work. The only benefit of her dunking was that the client knew her and knew she'd be "staking out" his home, so wasn't likely to call the cops on her. And he'd offered her access to his bathroom. Woo-hoo!

That evening she sent her cousins off, insisting Diego needed to spend the evening with his family, and Tito could rest up for their next day clean-up. They protested, but she convinced them she could handle things.

No one would attempt the vandalism until after dark. Too many people in this neighborhood walked their dogs, or with their spouses, or drove in and out during daylight and dusk hours. But after dark only javelinas, bobcats, bats, or those up to no good ventured out.

Before it got totally dark, she moved her lawn chair and equipment to the side of the house. And settled in for a long, lonely wait.

As the dusk grew thicker, Madrone felt the weight of responsibility on her shoulders. It was clear that the tagger was acquainted with Diego and Tito, well enough to know their former graffiti signature. He or she wasn't targeting any of the cousins' competitors, or at least the competitors weren't sharing that information with them. That narrowed the motive down to revenge or money.

She wriggled in the chair, failing to get comfortable. Face it. She didn't need to deduce a motive if she could catch the perpetrator in the act. The cops could take over from there.

Unless. Unless the police didn't believe her part of the story. She needed to be very stealthy and get a photo of the person actually spraying the tag on and then tackle him or her. She should have figured this out earlier, and asked Tito to stick around. But no, she had to do it all by herself. Didn't want to rely on a man. Even when another set of eyes and another body could have been a big help.

She sighed. She'd gulp down her ridiculous pride and ask for help. She picked up her cell phone and texted Tito.

His response came in moments— "Pretty busy right now. Catch up with you soon."

She texted back. "I should have asked for your help. Two will work better than one."

"Two works better for lots of things. Catch the drift?"

She blushed. No one to see it, so why care? But she did. Was it Tito's words or her failure to ask for help earlier that embarrassed her?

Didn't matter now. What mattered was getting help. She phoned Diego. His wife Diana answered, breathless. Not again!

Madrone asked to speak to Diego. "He's out. Some business meeting or other. My man is always busy."

So. She was on her own. She'd figure it out. She usually did.

As it grew darker, it became harder to stay awake. Madrone nodded, slapped her face, splashed some of her drinking water on her cheeks and neck, stood up and paced.

Velvety dark, dark as only Tucson, the Dark-Sky Association headquarters, with its severe restrictions on nighttime illumination, could be. Silent. She checked her phone for the time: 1:30 a.m. Tagging time?

Half an hour or so later, she heard the sound of gravel crunching at the front of the house. She sniffed the air. If the noise came from a javelina or a bunch of javelinas, she'd smell them for sure. The wild peccaries smelled worse than old garbage with a skunky aroma distinctly their own. Camera in one hand, long twist ties in her pocket, she crept close to the corner. Heard the hiss of a spray can. She moved silently, thankful they'd left the gate open.

There! She saw a shadowy form crouched near the corner. She held up her camera, aimed and shot a burst of pictures. The flash went off, and the game was on! The tagger rose from a crouch and turned to face Madrone, who dropped the camera and leapt at the tagger.

The tagger aimed the spray can at Madrone's face, but aimed too low. Madrone crossed the ten feet between them in seconds and thrust her arms against a solid form, shorter than her but sturdy. The tagger fell back against the wall and shoved off toward Madrone, flinging the spray can at her and spinning toward the driveway and freedom. Madrone caught the can against her chest, clutched it, and dashed after the tagger.

She tripped on a small duffel and sprawled forward, breaking her fall with her hands—palms spread—and forearms, twisting to fall on her side. Thank heavens for judo training in her teens. She let the momentum of the fall help her bounce up and keep running after the vandal. Who was heading rocket-fast down the drive and into the street.

Madrone ran faster, determined not to let this creep escape. The tagger slowed and veered toward the side of the road. In seconds, a bicycle started off down the street. Madrone stopped, defeated.

Then she heard a thump, a cry of terror and a crashing noise, followed by cursing in English and Spanish.

She hurried to see what had happened, but the spill had slowed her.

"I've got to see if the tagger is hurt, if they need help," she said to the night sky. "Maybe I can still catch them."

Instead of the expected silence, a familiar voice said, "She'll be okay. The bike, maybe not." Tito appeared, clutching the arm of a young woman wearing a hoodie. She wriggled and twisted in a fruitless attempt to get away.

"Hey, Madrone," Tito said. "Looks like your stakeout worked."

Diego strolled up the drive, rolling a battered bicycle beside him. "Good job, Cuz." He pulled his phone from a pocket and aimed the flash at her. "You really get into your work."

She looked down at her body. Her overalls and T-shirt were bright teal blue. "That's about the same color I'm gonna be by tomorrow," she predicted. "I tripped. Already feel the bruises forming."

"We saw," Tito said. "Once you got up, we went after the tagger."

"I thought you might be really mad if we came to help you instead of grabbing your target," Diego said. "Seriously, do you need an ambulance?"

"I'm the one needs first aid," said the tagger. "I could sue all three of you."

"The cops will help you. I called them." Diego moved closer to the tagger. "Are you . . . Emma?" Diego asked. "Emma from Tucson High way back when?"

"You two should know better than to take somebody else's territory. My brothers and me have a painting biz that's better than yours and you're horning in on the good neighborhoods. I had to stop it."

"Tell me she's not the blue-haired girl from your youth," Madrone said.

Tito laughed. "None other."

~*~

MARIACHI MISCHIEF

AMBRE LEFFLER

Gustavo, the ghost, drifted across the bar at the Fox Theatre on Congress in downtown Tucson. In two hours the quiet would be interrupted. He heard the lock turn in the front door. Moments later the manager Gloria walked in, carrying a large eegee's cup. Gustavo inhaled the tart lime scent. He floated behind her to get a better whiff. Lucky Lime had been his favorite eegee's flavor. If only he could take one more sip.

Gloria shivered. "It's cold in here. Who turned on the air conditioning in March?" She set down the cup and made her way toward the office, keys clanking. Gustavo hovered above the straw. It wasn't fair, being trapped in the theatre. He dove for the cup, sending it tumbling over.

The manager returned to the lobby. "What the..." She picked up the cup, heaved a sigh, and disappeared behind the bar. She reappeared with a damp cloth. "How did that tip over?"

"How did what tip over?" Gloria's assistant manager, Dawn, walked through the door.

"My Lucky Lime. I went to turn off the air conditioning and when I came back it was knocked over."

Dawn raised her eyebrows. "Probably Gustavo."

Gloria shook her head. "I don't believe in ghosts."

Gustavo folded his arms and scowled. He drifted into the

theatre. "Let's see if you still don't believe in ghosts after tonight."

The band arrived to do a sound check. Gustavo floated among them, watching hopefully as they unpacked their instrument cases. Two electric guitars. A drum set. Two keyboards. No trumpet, violin, or vihuela. He sighed in disappointment. As he returned to the bar he hummed "Volver Volver" quietly to himself.

The lines were long for the sold out show. Gustavo drifted below the bar. He yanked one of the soda lines free. Shouts from the bartender as club soda sprayed everywhere told Gustavo this was a success. He flew up to the ceiling to look down on the mess. The bartender was mopping up the counter while apologizing to customers and offering them napkins to clean up.

Dawn glanced over at Gloria.

"It was just a busted line. We're behind on maintenance. Don't give me that look."

Loud applause signaled the start of the concert. A guitar riff reverberated clear out to the lobby. Gustavo tried to plug his ears, but it was futile. He soared up to the catwalk and found the spotlight aimed at the lead guitarist. Giving it a nudge, he aimed it right in the guy's face. The guitarist put up his hand to block the light and missed the next few chords. Gustavo smiled.

It didn't last long. The guitarist turned his back toward his band and started jamming. The audience loved it, cheering for more. Gustavo huffed and drifted down to the speakers by the stage. Time for his next move. He rummaged for a microphone off stage left. He plugged it in, then held it right against the speakers. The screeching and echoing high pitch were worse than nails on a chalkboard.

The band switched off their amps, looking puzzled at each other. The sound board technician held up her hands and shrugged. The audience booed. Gustavo clapped his hands and returned to his usual spot in the projection booth. The show went on, but everyone was on edge.

Gloria and Dawn closed later than usual after handling all the customer complaints and the band demanding answers.

"I don't get it. They did a full sound check and everything was fine. And who would be up on the catwalk? The lighting crew would have seen someone."

Dawn whispered "It was—"

"It was not a ghost. I don't care what the legend says, or the stories, or whatever. We'll just have to be better prepared for the next show. Thank God it's body builders and not a band."

***

If there was anything Gustavo despised more than rock bands, it was body builders. The cloying smell of that baby oil. Ugh. And the glitter. It always made him sneeze. Not to mention the preening and ridiculous costumes with all that bared flesh. Nothing like the dignified charro pants with metal buttons down the sides and the short-waisted jackets of mariachi.

Gustavo took a long nap to prepare for the evening. The overpowering oily sweet smell woke him up. It was worse than ever. They seemed to be putting on twice as much to make up for the missed show last year. Glitter in vivid pinks, peacock blues, and emerald greens spilled over on the counters. Gustavo sneezed. No one heard him over the techno music blasting in the dressing room. He winced at the awful sound.

He made a diving pass over the counter, tipping over as many baby oil bottles as he could. He then doubled back and went for the glitter jars. It created a nightmare of a sticky mess. The body builders accused each other of being clumsy and knocking over the various jars and bottles.

Gloria rushed in to see why everyone was yelling. She cursed when she saw the glitter and oil cascading over the counter and oozing over the floor. This was going to be a beast to clean up, and a liability if anyone slipped on the slick oil. She ran back to the office and grabbed the floor mats they used at the entrance during monsoon season. Returning to the dressing room, she switched off the music and instructed the body builders to wipe their feet on the mats before going backstage.

Gustavo flew ahead to the men's restroom by the bar, one of his favorite haunts. He shook off the oil and green glitter he'd inadvertently flown through on his dive across the counter. He smelled like a mix of baby's breath and vegetable oil, but it was worth it. The staff would have to see now that they were booking the wrong kind of entertainment.

***

A light breeze moved through Gustavo. He floated above the roof of the Fox Theatre. The sweet smell of grilled tortillas drifted up to him, followed closely by the smoky adobada scent of al pastor. He closed his eyes at the memory of street tacos. They fit just right in his hand, crispy bites of tortilla giving way to juicy shreds of pork. It was the perfect pre-concert meal.

The stars were out, visible in the metropolitan dark sky city. A concert started up down the street at the Rialto Theatre. Gustavo braced himself for the onslaught of brash guitars and artless drumming. But then he heard the legato notes of the trumpet echoing across the night sky. He flew over to the corner closest to the sound.

His heart swelled; his eyes brimmed with tears. He lifted his fingers and pressed the valves to the trumpet he imagined holding to his lips. He was suddenly back next to Jimmy on the six-string bass and Olivia on violin. They were tuning up before their gig at El Charro Café. He loved the traditional songs the best, though it was fun to play customer requests too.

He opened his eyes when he heard a drum. What was this music? He hovered above the marquee and peered down the street until he saw the sign that said Calexico. It wasn't true mariachi, but the trumpeter knew how to play. Gustavo shimmied to the beat during the fast songs and swayed during the slow ones. He grew restless when the trumpet stopped playing and slipped through an air duct to return inside.

Gustavo longed to hear mariachi again, to feel the vibrations of the vihuela strings, to hear the tuning special to this music. He needed to get the attention of Gloria. She seemed to be the one in charge. But she didn't believe he existed. He'd have to ramp

178

up his antics to show her that these shows she lined up were not the right ones for his city.

***

A low rumbling jarred Gustavo out of his sleep. What…was… that. He sped-flew into the theatre. Oh no. No, no, no. A long low wavelength passed through his being. It jumbled everything, same as when he had a human form and it made his stomach upset. The Wurlitzer organ tuner was here. Sheer torture. He thought he'd thoroughly checked the schedule. He would have stayed on the roof if he'd known.

An aisle door opened. Gloria strode in with a clipboard. She made her way down toward the stage to the tuner.

"Thank you for working us in. We've had some equipment issues so I wanted to make sure everything was in good shape."

"What kind of issues?"

"Oh, feedback with the speakers, lights being moved, that kind of thing."

"I see. So, Gustavo is still haunting the place, huh?"

Gloria sighed. "There are no such things as ghosts. It's just kids playing pranks or faulty equipment."

"The legend of the ghost at the Fox Theatre is a big part of local tradition. Are you doing the ghost tours this year?"

"Yes, but only because it sells tickets. Anyway, let me know when you wrap up here."

"Will do." The tuner swiveled back to the organ.

Gustavo fumed. He was going to have to take care of this first, then get back to the problem at hand. He floated out to the bar to get the necessary supplies. There wasn't a matinee so the bartender wouldn't be here in the afternoon. Gustavo stocked up on bar towels and popcorn. Then he slipped behind the wall on stage right to wait for the tuner to leave.

***

There was always a hum in the audience before the house lights went down. This excited Gustavo, the moments of anticipation. Tonight he had another reason to be excited. The first few notes of the organ warbled through the theatre. As the piece expanded, so did the range of notes. The organist hit the lowest note which came out as a wheezing muffled sound.

Gustavo did a back flip in celebration. His plan was working.

The audience murmured. The organist continued. What was supposed to be a treble note blurted out like a foghorn. The audience noise rose up a notch. After reaching the end of the piece, the curtain closed. Gloria walked to center stage and announced intermission to address a technical issue.

She batted at the curtain to find the seam and stomped backstage. "We just had this tuned. What is wrong?"

A stagehand left to inspect the pipes. He returned a few minutes later. "I found these in the pipes." He set down a pile of bar towels and several handfuls of popcorn.

"How did those get in there? Who would do this? Why? And if anyone says the ghost did it, you're fired. Flick the lights to let the audience know intermission is over."

Gustavo's shoulders drooped. He thought for sure this would get through to Gloria. His only consolation was that half the audience returned. The rest lined up at the box office demanding refunds. When offered a ticket for a future show, several customers said they heard the place was haunted and wouldn't be back.

Gustavo was happy they at least acknowledged his presence. Though it hurt his feelings that they didn't want to be at the theatre because of him. It was just some harmless pranks. And he really wanted them to experience good music, not this racket that rattled his nerves on the weekends.

Gloria called a staff meeting for the next day. "We can't keep having these things go wrong. Ticket sales are dropping and we had to issue a lot of refunds tonight. A reporter from the Arizona Daily Star called to ask if it was true the ghost was creating mischief here." Gloria closed her eyes and rubbed her temples. "I'll see all of you tomorrow at noon."

The staff grumbled as they closed up. Gustavo could hear snatches of conversation.

"She doesn't believe in ghosts."

"I had to tell customers maybe it was a mouse. That didn't go over well."

"What will we do about the fundraising gala?"

When it was quiet again, he drifted over to the display case in the lobby with historic photographs. In the center was the mariachi band he played with in the 1950s. Jimmy was in center. Gustavo was next to him, holding his trumpet. Olivia held her violin off to the right. He floated for a long time in front of her image. She was so beautiful, with long graceful fingers.

Gustavo sighed. Memories of concerts, weddings, and quinceañeras passed by. He glanced at the other guitarists and then looked at the reflection of his image.

How did he get trapped in this theatre? The others passed before he did, their instruments silenced. He longed to hear their music. The local culture seemed to forget the rich history, the stories told in their songs. Gustavo learned the songs from his father, who learned them from his father back in Mexico. With no one to play this music, their legacy would disappear.

A drip, drip, drip sound shook Gustavo out of his reverie. He didn't realize he'd been weeping. He wiped away one tear and traced a heart on the glass around the photograph. Then he floated up to the roof. Downtown was quiet. A gecko scurried after moths drawn to the buzzing lights of the marquee. The pungently sweet fragrance of orange blossoms wafted up to him. He didn't know what he was going to do next. All he knew was that he was completely alone.

***

The creak of the side door woke up Gustavo. Lights flicked on. He slowly made his way toward the lobby. Gloria was arranging Sonoran hot dogs on a table. Gustavo circled around her. He saw Gloria shiver.

"Boo!" Gustavo waved a hand in front of Gloria's face. Nothing. Gustavo huffed. Gloria's bangs drifted up in the draft. She frowned and looked up toward the air conditioning vent. Other staff members arrived. She turned and greeted them, gesturing toward the hot dogs. Once they filled their plates, she started the meeting.

"Okay. We need to come up with a win for the fundraising gala. The entertainment needs to be spectacular, something to bring the community together and draw a crowd. There's a lot of competition and we all know about the cutbacks in funding for the arts."

Everyone mumbled around the table. Gustavo nodded from his perch in the chandelier.

"Who has an idea?"

"What about a puppeteer? That would be cool."

"Yeah, if you're five years old."

"Do you have a better idea?"

"The magician from last fall was amazing. People were asking for a second show."

Gloria shook her head. "He's booked through next year. What else?"

Everyone looked down at the table.

"Look, I'm not going to sugar coat this. If we don't raise a significant amount of money, the Fox Theatre will be closing."

Gustavo gasped. The staff members stared at Gloria.

"What do you mean, closing? Like, permanently?"

"Yes, permanently. I don't need to spell out how tough the last two years have been. And with the recent pranks around here the customers have dwindled."

"You mean the gho—"

Gloria lifted an eyebrow. "You remembered just in time what I said about mentioning ghosts."

"But what if we make the, erm, spirit a showcase? Maybe ramp up the ghost tours? Or have a ghost hunter come in! We could live stream it and charge for the link."

Gustavo shrank back. He couldn't breathe. Everyone said ghost hunters were fakes, but he didn't want to find out if they were real.

"One more suggestion like that and you really will be fired. Dawn, you've been quiet."

"I was thinking that it would be fun to have a throwback to local history. It would draw in a multi-generational audience."

"That's an interesting idea. Any thoughts on a specific time period?"

"Well, we could do something from the time the Fox Theatre was founded, but I think that was done just a few years ago. I'd have to do some research on what other bands were notable that played here."

Gloria stood up. "What about the photographs in the display case? There might be an idea there."

They all moved into the lobby, stopping in front of the case where Gustavo had wept the night before.

"Does... anyone else see a heart shape traced in the glass?" someone asked tentatively.

Murmurs of "yes" affirmed what he saw.

Gloria heaved a sigh. "Kids. There were lots of kids at the show last night."

Gustavo flew over and hovered between Gloria's and Dawn's shoulders. This was it! They would see the photograph and finally bring back mariachi. Dawn leaned in and studied it.

"What do you all think about—"

"Hey, a tribute band would work! You know, something that would appeal to everyone and be rated okay for the kids. They wouldn't charge as much, either."

Everyone talked over each other with their favorite tribute band concerts. Gloria finally had to shout to be heard.

"Okay, I think we have a winner. I'll look into availability and offer a contract. Let's hope this works. Otherwise, it will be the final event at the Fox."

The staff members cleared out. Dawn stayed to help Gloria clean up.

"Are you serious, that the Fox might close?"

"Yes. The grant money we'd applied for didn't come through. There were a lot more applications this year. Not a surprise."

"It would really be too bad to see all this history boarded up."

The two women locked the doors. The thought of being alone forever send a shiver through Gustavo. He didn't think the tribute band would be a big success. He knew mariachi would bring people together and remind them of the stories from Tucson's heritage. He came so close to seeing his dream come true. But then it evaporated.

***

Gustavo drooped along the bar. He halfheartedly flicked a few popcorn kernels at the bartender. The bartender didn't even look up. Gustavo drifted by the tap, tipping over two cups of beer before floating to Gloria's office. He didn't see the point of pulling his usual pranks. Soon he would have no one here to play with.

He slipped through the keyhole to see if anything interesting was happening. Gloria wasn't in. The whirr of the fax machine spooked Gustavo. He turned and hovered over the page as it rolled out. Scanning the document, he saw it was a contract for the tribute band. He realized this was actually going to happen.

Gustavo rolled up the contract and carried it into the theatre where he stuffed it down the C# organ pipe. There. He drifted into the projection booth and studied the audience filtering in. He would miss their chatter, the mix of perfumes with beer and popcorn. It wasn't their fault they had poor taste in entertainment. They just hadn't experienced mariachi.

The hum increased as more patrons found their seats. Gustavo drifted back to the lobby. Gloria hurried across the red carpet, grumbling. A ticket taker asked where she'd been.

"I got a flat tire. Didn't anyone get my text?"

The ticket taker shook his head.

"How is everything going? Did that contract get faxed over?"

"Everything is going smoothly. I checked the fax and nothing came in."

"You'd think they would want this gig. I'll send an e-mail to follow up. There's not much time to arrange travel."

The ticket taker nodded, then returned to his post at the theatre entrance. Gustavo made a note to keep tabs on any incoming emails. He didn't have Gloria's password, but he had a plan.

***

For the next few days Gustavo floated just below the ceiling any time Gloria was in the office. He watched her type the e-mail to the band's manager asking why they hadn't received the signed contract. Two days later he heard the ping of an incoming message and saw the subject line about the contract before Gloria did. He floated down next to the cup of coffee by the keyboard. Gustavo made a calculated flick to send coffee spilling over onto the keys.

Gloria muttered a string of curses, grabbing a tissue to try and mop it up. She stood up and flung open the office door. Gustavo listened for her footsteps heading in the direction of the bar. He quickly deleted any trace of the message. He breezed just above her as she stomped back in.

Gloria mopped up the mess and threw the towel to the side of the desk, narrowly missing Gustavo. He hovered above her right shoulder as she logged back into her e-mail. He let out a small sigh as he saw the inbox free of messages from the tribute band. Gloria rubbed the back of her neck where the hairs stood slightly on end. She shook her head and continued reading messages.

Gustavo smiled for the first time in days. This part of the plan was working. Now he just needed to keep an ear out for phone calls. He drifted out into the hallway. Dawn walked right under him. She was humming something quietly. He turned and hovered above her left ear to catch more. He nearly rolled over when he heard the familiar rhythm of "Guantanamera." She knew mariachi music! Gustavo had been focusing on the wrong person.

He remembered now that Dawn had been looking closely at the photograph the day of the planning meeting. She was about to say something before everyone got excited about a tribute band. If he could only direct her attention back to mariachi, there was a chance she'd remember her idea from the photograph. Then she might suggest mariachi instead. A zing sizzled through all of Gustavo's particles. He had to get her attention. He just wasn't sure how.

***

Brrring…brrring… This annoying sound interrupted Gustavo's nap in the chandelier. When he realized it was the phone, he zoomed into Gloria's office just in time to hear her say "Finally. I was beginning to think you didn't want this gig." Silence, then "I didn't receive the fax." More silence. "I didn't receive your e-mail either. I don't know what happened. Why don't you send the fax again while I am right here."

Gustavo tried not to panic. There wasn't a convenient cup of coffee near the keyboard this time. He swooped below the desk and yanked out every cable in sight. The fax machine and computer monitor blinked off.

"Oh, come on. You've got to be kidding me. I'm beginning to think this whole thing is cursed."

Gustavo smothered a laugh.

"Not that I believe in ghosts." Gloria pointed at the ceiling.

Gustavo floated in front of Gloria's face for a moment, then decided it wasn't worth it. He was drifting toward the door when her cell phone rang.

"Gloria speaking." She frowned at the voice on the other end. "Our fax and phone lines just went down. I'm sorry to miss your message again."

Gustavo heard a man's voice increase in volume.

"No, we really do want to book you for our gala. Let me call you back in an hour after I get everything up and running. I promise—"

The man cut her off, speaking rapidly. It sounded like he was going through a long list.

"I assure you, this place isn't haunted. We had a few freak glitches but our technicians are quick to get things back on track."

Gloria pressed the phone to her ear. The man stopped talking. A second later he ended the connection. She threw the phone on the desk. "Great. Just great. Now what?"

Dawn passed by the door office. "Is... everything okay?"

"No. The band just cancelled."

"What? Why?"

"They said we never responded to their fax or e-mail. They were just about to send the fax again when the fax line and Internet connection went out. Now they believe the rumors that the Fox Theatre is haunted and their show will be a disaster with unexplained technical glitches."

Dawn leaned against the wall and crossed her arms over her chest. "What do we do now?"

"I don't know. Maybe we can find a local act. We need to come up with a winning idea by the weekend or we'll be finished."

Gustavo swirled around Dawn's head. She shivered.

"Dawn, what is it? It looked like a shadow just passed across your face."

"I was trying to remember an idea I had at the meeting. But it flitted past before I could catch it."

"Well if you remember be sure to write it down."

Dawn sighed. "I definitely will. If it returns."

***

Gustavo spent the rest of the day thinking of ways to jog Dawn's memory of her idea. She seemed to like "Guantanamera." He would have to create an instrument. Floating behind the bar, he filled a souvenir cup halfway with ice. He fitted another empty cup over the top, then shook it. He ducked behind the bar to wait.

The box office team drifted in and gathered around the bar. Perfect. Gustavo waited to hear Dawn's voice, then started shaking the ice cups like maracas. Shake shake shake shake shake. He smiled at the rhythm. So many happy memories of his trumpet soaring above the strumming guitars at either side of him. He repeated the phrase, this time with more gusto.

"Did someone hear that?" One of the team members spoke up.

"I heard something. Maybe the ice machine is out of order again. It was making a grinding sound yesterday."

Gustavo levitated above the bar to see if Dawn was listening. He tried again. Shake shake shake shake shake. He saw her tap her fingers to the rhythm. It was working!

"I'll put in a work order. I'm suddenly craving Mexican food. Does anyone want to go pick up something from Street Taco before the box office opens?"

"Count me in."

Gustavo wilted as he watched Dawn leave. He dropped the cups in the bar sink and wafted up to the theatre balcony. He thought for sure his plan would work. He gazed down at the stage, reflecting on all the memories of concerts he'd played here. And concerts he'd heard, too. The theatre was rich in its history of musical acts. And it was all about to disappear, like he had.

***

Two teenagers whispered to each other as the house lights dimmed.

"I can't wait for this concert. I've been listening to all his songs on my playlist for weeks."

"Me too."

Gustavo floated over their heads and saw the screen of a cell phone with the songs listed. Playlist. Cell phone. This could be the answer. He would need to create one last big distraction to make it work.

The next day he lingered in the box office. Dawn always came in early. She flicked on the lights, whistling as she set down her cell phone. Gustavo patiently waited until there was a ping for a message. Dawn picked up the phone to read it, then set it back down. He'd have to act fast. He picked up a box of staples and threw them into the hallway.

"What was that?" Dawn got up and quickly walked out the door.

Gustavo turned and found her music app. He downloaded a playlist with the best of mariachi and took the phone with him as he whooshed out the door, down the hall, and into the theatre. He tapped the screen every few seconds to keep it unlocked. Once in the theatre, he connected the phone to the amp and hit play.

"Guantanamera" boomed through the theatre. The entire staff ran into the theatre to see who was playing the music. Gustavo ghost-played the trumpet, though no one could see or hear him.

"What kind of prank is this?" one of the box office team members said as he strode toward the amp. He turned to Dawn. "How did your phone get here?"

"I don't know. Wait—" Dawn held up her hand. "I've had that song in my head for days, ever since the planning meeting. Oh, that was my idea! We should have a mariachi band for the gala. We could tie it in to the Fox Theatre's birthday. It would bring in all ages, appeal to multiple generations, and create a bond with the community."

She looked hopefully at the others. Gustavo felt like he might vaporize soon if someone didn't speak.

Gloria nodded. "I think that's a great idea. Mariachis are a significant part of Tucson's cultural identity. We could involve the schools, too. Get me a list by this afternoon and I'll start making some calls."

Gustavo thought he might just float clear out of the theatre. His dream was coming true.

***

The mariachi band got there at 3:00 for a sound check. Gustavo hovered above a front row seat, giddy with happiness.

189

When he heard the trumpet, he was home.

The evening was a smashing success. Tucsonans attended the gala in record numbers. Schoolchildren pointed out to their parents the instruments they were learning. Couples clapped their hands to the rhythms. Grandparents sang along to the traditional songs. The mariachi gave an encore of "Las Mañanitas" in honor of the Fox Theatre's birthday.

Gustavo felt a strong breeze waft along his sides. It wasn't until he looked down that he realized he had drifted out of the theatre. He was free. Finally free. He heard a whistle and saw his bandmates waiting for him under a palo verde tree. They clapped their hands to the rhythm. Gustavo joined them, his heart dancing to the beat of the mariachi.

ABOUT THE AUTHORS

JANET ALCORN is a librarian who launched a lifelong dream by Googling, "how to write a novel," on a slow afternoon at work. Since that fateful day, her short stories have been published in the 2021 Deathlehem anthology, the Storyteller Series podcast, and the Arizona Authors Association annual literary magazine. When she isn't wrangling cantankerous fictional people or earning a living, Janet gardens, listens to 80s rock at ear-bleeding volume, and hangs out in Tucson with her husband and son. Learn more about Janet at janetalcorn.com or follow her on Twitter (@ja_alcorn) or Facebook (facebook.com/authorjanetalcorn).

MARY BALL is a former computer scientist who has written a cozy mystery which she was fine-tuning, plus working on a collection of short stories when she became a full-time caregiver for her mother and father-in-law. That was five years ago. She is just now getting back to writing. Her goal is to finish editing the collection of short stories and the cozy mystery while creating new stories. It isn't easy to get back into a writing routine after five years, but she is trying. The Devil is in the Details is her first effort in this new period of her life.

SUSAN CUMMINS MILLER, Tucson author, a former field

geologist and college instructor, writes the Frankie MacFarlane, Geologist, mysteries and the Keridec Rees historical mysteries. She compiled and edited A Sweet, Separate Intimacy: Women Writers of the American Frontier, 1800-1922, and recently released two poetry collections, Making Silent Stones Sing and Deciphering the Desert: a book of poems. Her poems, short stories, and essays appear frequently in journals and anthologies. Currently, she's working on Right of Capture, the seventh Frankie MacFarlane mystery, set in southwestern Arizona and Sonora, Mexico. www.susancumminsmiller.com

CONDA DOUGLAS, Conda's story, Triple Dang, is based on a too-memorable experience in a bar from when she lived in Tucson. She'll never reveal the bar's name, for Arizona is an Open Carry state. She loves Tucson, remembering fondly the scorpions, the monsoon lightning strikes, and even the tiny sidewinder on the front patio. Nowadays, Conda works on her Starke Dead Mysteries series. The ski resort town of Starke is, ahem, Sun Valley, Idaho where Conda grew up. She changed the name to protect her not-so-innocent friends and family.

For more on Conda and her writings, including her short stories, visit her Amazon page, https://amazon.com/author/condadouglas.

AMBRE LEFFLER writes to build community, nurture a deep connection with nature, and explore a mystery. She loves connecting patterns in music, stories, and nature. Ambre believes storytelling is the most powerful way to create meaningful change in ourselves and our relationships with other living beings.

Ambre is also a certified Breath Qigong Yoga and Tai Chi instructor. She composes silly songs for her three rescue cats. Her stack of books to be read include mysteries, historical fiction, and anything about nature, especially trees. Learn more about Ambre's writing and wellness practices for writers at her website ambredawnleffler.com.

JEFFREY J. MARIOTTE is the award-winning author of dozens of books, including the Major Crimes Squad: Phoenix procedural thriller series, historical Western epic Blood and Gold: The Legend of Joaquin Murrieta (with Peter Murrieta), the Cody Cavanaugh Western series, Tarzan and the Forest of Stone, and many more in various genres. He's also known for his comics and graphic novel work, especially long-running Weird Western series Desperadoes. He lives in the desert with his wife Marsheila Rockwell and their family.

KATHY McINTOSH, with a dark past as a high-tech marketer and columnist on words, Kathy McIntosh has translated her love of words, humor, nature, and great food into her fiction. She lives in southeastern Arizona., generally avoiding cactus spines.

Kathy's first two novels are humorous romps in the wilds of north Idaho, her former home. Her new Adventure Calls series about an ecotourism company is—so far—set in Arizona. The sleuth in her story, Madrone, features in the series. Learn more about Kathy and her award-winning short stories and novels at www.KathyMcIntosh.com.

KRIS NERI writes the humorous Tracy Eaton mysteries, featuring the daughter of eccentric Hollywood stars, the Samantha Brennan & Annabelle Haggerty magical series, featuring a questionable psychic who teams up with a goddess/FBI agent, along with thrillers and short stories. Some sixty-plus of her stories have been published in the US and overseas, and she's a two-time Pushcart Prize and a two-time Derringer Award winner for short fiction. Kris teaches writing for the Writers' Program of the UCLA Extension School. She makes her home in Silver City, NM. Readers are invited to visit her website: krisneri.com.

LYNN NICHOLAS, Lynn's first novel, Dancing Between the Beats, debuted in December, 2019. Inspiration for her writing springs from perceptive and often humorous observations of everyday life. Publication credits include Flash Fiction Magazine, Foliate Oak Literary Magazine, The Storyteller, The Wild Word, Every Day Fiction, Wow! Women on Writing, Sandsript Art & Literary Magazine, and others. Lynn lacks the most basic of mechanical skills, but can create awesome meals, grow an English-style desert garden, and connect with animals on an instinctive level. Lynn is a member of Sisters in Crime and the Society of Southwestern Authors.

EMMA PEREZ, Emma Pérez's first novel, Gulf Dreams, was published in 1996 and is the first Chicanx queer/lesbian novels in print. Her second novel, Forgetting the Alamo, Or, Blood Memory (2009) earned awards including the Christopher Isherwood Writing Grant (2009). Her mystery, Electra's Complex (2015), takes place at a college and a history professor is the protagonist. A collection of previously published essays and poems, Queering the Border, is forthcoming in Spring 2023 and a dystopic novella, Testimony of a Shifter), detailing the lives of sex-shifting rebels resisting a corrupt global order, is forthcoming in 2023. She lives in Tucson.

ELAINE A. POWERS, originally from Peoria, IL, currently resides in Tucson, AZ. After a career as a laboratory biologist, she is now pursuing her dream of writing science-based children's books, murder mysteries and audio theatre scripts. Elaine continues her work as a citizen scientist for iguana conservation, serving on the IUCN Iguana Specialist Group. She is a founding member of the Tucson Sisters in Crime chapter and President of the Tucson Poetry Society. For more information, visit her website www.elaineapowers.com as well as the publisher's webpage www.lyricpower.net. She also has original videos on her YouTube Channel Curtis Curly-tail Speaks https://www.youtube.com/channel/UCG4iBd2NLDlHcOwCOEneGVQ

MINERVA RAZ lives and writes in Tucson, Arizona and Hood River, Oregon. Her fiction and poetry have been published in various literary magazines. She is working on her first novel, a modern gothic exploration of family secrets, deceit and redemption. When she's not writing, Minerva is busy immersing herself in nature-hiking, kayaking, snow shoeing, and gardening.

CYNTHIA SABELHAUS is the editor of Calliope, the journal of the American Mensa Writers' Special Interest Group. Her short stories have appeared in anthologies, including Seascape: Best New England Crime Stories and Malice Domestic 16: Mystery Most Diabolical. Cynthia lives in Southern Arizona with her writer-husband, Bud. She is currently working on a novel.

ELENA E. SMITH has appeared in the anthologies Love Kills, BOULD Awards 2022, and Darkness Brewing, and has had short stories published in Yellow Mama Magazine and Kings River Life Magazine. She plans to self-publish her first novel in 2023.

PATRICK WHITEHURST writes both fiction and nonfiction, the latter of which includes the books "Haunted Monterey County" and "Murder and Mayhem in Tucson." His stories range from true crime to thriller fiction reminiscent of Tales from the Crypt. Patrick's writing can be found in Punk Noir, Shotgun Honey, Pulp Modern, Hoosier Noir, Adrenaline Shot Comics, and Switchblade Magazine. He's been featured in the anthologies "Bitter Chills," "Wild Violence," and elsewhere. Find him on Instagram @ whitehurst12 or at patrickwhitehurst.com.

EVA ELDRIDGE: EDITOR, resides in the Sonoran desert where she investigates ways to stay cool during the summer. Traveling to cooler climates is one of the ways Eva manages to avoid the heat but she always returns to the desert where she enjoys gardening, shopping at the local farmers market, and working as a telecommunications engineer. She lives with her husband, a pushy dog. Eva writes for Big Blend Magazine, http://www.bigblendnetwork.com and has been published in SandScript. Her website can be found at http://evaeldridge.com.

Made in USA - North Chelmsford, MA
1358214_9798375928050
02.06.2023 1522